I0519652

The Land of the Eagle Feathers
The Book of Summer

By

Joe G. Morin & Jo Ann Bullard

Edited by June Haney Henley

Copyright© 2018

Published by

Lyrics and Books from the Heart
Publishing Company, Inc.

2018

Preface

You have to look deep, way below the anger, the hurt, the hate, the jealousy, the self-pity, way down deeper where the dreams lie, son. Find your dream. It's the pursuit of the dream that heals you.   Billy Mills

The Keepers of the Yawi continue their quest. They must find the second book, *The Book of Summer,* to save The Land of the Eagle Feathers. They will use the clues found in *The Book of Spring* to locate the book in The Land of the Eagle Feathers.

They have lost their leader to the mysterious Unspeakables. Nobody has ever been able to rescue anyone from these powerful spirits. To save him, they must rely on a dangerous enemy leader, David. He wants the books for himself. They must trust him as well as two female mercenaries, Shanna and Angela, to rescue him. They have joined the group as well.

This assorted group must trust each other or die trying. Nobody fully trusts each other. Everyone keeps changing based on which wolf is dominant that day. Finding their leader will be no easy task. Finding *The Book of Summer,* using the clues from *The Book of Spring,* will even be harder.

There will be lots of surprises. There will be deception. There will be trials ahead for the group. Their enemies are more dangerous. Failure is not an option for them! It's too late to turn back!

- Will their mystical and magical skills be enough?
- Will they find their leader?
- Will they find *The Book of Summer*?
- Will they defeat the assassins sent to kill them?
- Will everyone survive?

Table of Contents

Chapter I
We need to find John:
Can we trust David?

It was just beginning to get light. The mountain forest was in full bloom. Spring comes late in the mountains. It would be summer in a few days. The Dogwoods that bordered the mountain trail were in full bloom. Their flowers were white with some pink. It was a ride through a tunnel of blossoms as a group of ten riders made their way through the mountain pass. The beauty of the mountains was in stark contrast to the dark thoughts of the riders.

Several members of this group had survived what was once thought impossible. They had found one of four sacred books of The Land of the Eagle Feathers: *The Book of Spring*. That journey, just a few months ago, almost cost them their very lives. Now they were embarking on the next part of their quest to find the next book: *The Book of Summer*. Would they survive this journey? The odds were not in their favor.

Their leader, John, had been kidnapped. They had to find him before they could even start to look for *The Book of Summer*. In order to do so, they would have to rely on and follow a vile man named David to rescue him. He was the only person that knew where to find John. This did not set well with them. David was not the only addition to the group. Angela, David's partner and bodyguard, and Shanna, another woman that they knew very little about, had joined the group as well. These three upset the balance of the group.

Soon they were out of the forest. The trail had become rocky with large boulders. The steep side of the mountain to the left side of the trail was dangerous. David was on the lead horse. He was followed by Moses, Mary, June, Nick, Rose, Antonio, Angela, Shanna and Lo Ming. Lo Ming was leading two pack mules behind her.

Rose could feel the discontent in the group. Much had happened in the past few weeks before they returned here. Nick and Rose had become very close on their first journey to The Land of the Eagle Feathers. Rose knew about Shanna. She had seen Shanna in her crystal ball with Nick two weeks ago. Shanna was Nick's first love. This really bothered her. Why was Shanna here? This was another part of the puzzle. Everything was changing. Rose had just found out that her first love was still alive. He was trapped somewhere in The Land of the Eagle Feathers. Everything about this land kept changing their lives.

Rose could feel that Nick was stressed about having Shanna here. This was not good, Rose thought. She knew he couldn't take much stress. Nick could feel Rose and Shanna looking at him. He didn't know how to handle the situation. He had started taking drugs again. He felt he needed them to get through each day.

The rest of the group had their own problems. Antonio was not in a good place. Angela was here with her boss, David. Antonio and Angela had been working together to double cross David. They wanted the books for themselves. Antonio worried if Angela was still on his side. He would have to be incredibly careful to get out of this alive. Mary was in a state of shock from the news she had heard about her having a son that was alive. She had thought her son had died in childbirth. Her father, David, was another problem for her. Could he had been responsible for telling her lies about her son? She didn't even know who the child's father was. She was in quite a fix because she had been working secretly with her father to take over The Land of the Eagle Feathers.

Moses was worried about Lo Ming. She seemed distant to him since their return from home. They had become lovers on their first trip to The Land of the Eagle Feathers. He could usually read her mind. She was blocking it for some reason.

He didn't know why Lo Ming was upset. Lo Ming was deep in thought. She had a secret. Lo Ming had taken the time to find out about Moses' family. She was shocked to find out about who his mother was. She and Moses' mother had met a long time ago. They shared the dark secret that she wouldn't want Moses to find out about.

June had other things on her mind. She was on this quest to find out about why The Land of the Eagle Feathers was so important for her tribe. She thought the Elders of her tribe were not totally truthful about what they had told her. One thing that did keep her going was One Feather. She knew that One Feather was going to be her husband one day. She only had to keep them alive.

There was only one thing that was keeping this group together. They had to rescue John, their leader. He was the only one that could keep the group together to find the other sacred books of The Land of the Eagle Feathers. It was becoming increasing clear that John had selected this group very carefully. They were all like pieces of a complex puzzle. Each of them was intertwined with each other. He must have worked on this for years.

They were genuinely concerned about who was leading them. David was not a person that could be trusted. They knew that he was only out for himself. He was not someone that you would trust to save your life. The only reason they followed him was that they needed him to find John.

As they started up the steep narrow pass of a mountain, Nick and June stopped their horses. They didn't like what they saw. This was a perfect place for an ambush. The trail was narrow with rocks and boulders above the trail. They could sense that people were watching them. David stopped his horse. He could sense them as well.

A small rock rolled down the cliff beside David's horse. This meant trouble. David immediately turned his black stallion around in the narrow trail. Behind him were nine riders followed by their pack mules. A large boulder came roaring down the mountainside. The horse in front of him suddenly turned and ran, knocking off his rider. The boulder would hit the man in a few seconds.

David spurred his horse and grabbed the man by his shoulders, half dragging the man down the mountain trail. The boulder just missed David's horse as it rolled down the mountainside taking several large pine trees with it. David dropped the man. He shouted for everyone to make a run for it. Other boulders soon followed. Dust was everywhere. The others were already down the trail. They had stopped under an outcropping for protection from the landside. David had made it just in time as the mountainside seemed to swallow the trail behind him. The others looked into the dust, hoping that Moses somehow had survived. They could see nothing but large boulders, rocks and trees blocking the trail.

David smiled to himself. This group before him was in a bad state of mind. Nobody seemed to totally trust the other person. Everyone had something to hide. This would work for his goal. He would try to pit people against each other. He would stir the pot. Nobody in this group was whom they seemed.

Lo Ming looked David squarely in his eyes and asked, "Where is Moses?" David replied, "He should be here shortly. He is too tough for a landside to get him." As David finished his reply, a dust covered man appeared out of the dust and rocks.

They knew it was Moses from the Australian Bush hat on his head. Moses walked up to them. Taking his hat, he brushed the dirt off his shirt and body. They asked him how did he survive? They had seen him fall off his horse. The only thing he said was, "David," much to the surprise of everyone there. That was the last thing anyone expected him to say. David was the one member of the group that nobody thought would save anyone, unless it was to his advantage. He was a very dangerous man.

Moses was confused. The David he knew would have left him for dead. Moses had a score to settle with David from long ago. Maybe, Moses would not kill him after this quest was completed. The rule of The Land of the Eagle Feathers was that if a man saved you, you were responsible to save that man in return. Moses wondered if this was part of David's plan. David was a very devious man. Did he save Moses to save himself or was there some sliver of good in David?

David looked at the group. "We will have to go another way to get there. We are running out of time if we are to rescue John. This other trail will not be easy. We will have to leave the horses in the meadow below. I hope you are all in shape for the climb ahead." With that said, he turned his horse and started back down the trail. David stopped his horse after a few feet. He turned and caught something in his hands. It was a black arrow. David yelled, "If you thought you could kill us this easy, Night Panther, you are a fool." David threw the arrow into the air, pointed at it, and it burst into flames. Then he spurred his horse toward the meadow below.

The group followed him down the mountain trail. Their thoughts were on what they had witnessed with David. They realized that David was a man not to take lightly. He had powers. The amount and type of powers were what they would like to know. Someday, they knew that they would have to face him. Would they be able to match his powers? Rose knew the answer to that question. She only hoped that they all stayed united. It would take all the group's special powers to match David's. After all, they were **The Keepers of the Yawi**.

It took the better part of the day to backtrack down the mountain trail to the grassy meadow. Everyone was disappointed to lose a day. David was, especially in a foul mood. He thought that he must be getting soft. In his younger days, he would have stayed and fought Night Panther's tribe. He would have crushed them like ants. He knew better than what he would had done in his rash youth. He couldn't take the chance of losing any of this group. Like it or not, he needed them to obtain the books for himself. He needed the books' powers. He had enemies. Some of them were close like his wife, Benita. Others were like Raven, his superior, that would like to eliminate him as a competitor for power within **The Omen**. He may control **The Dark Ones,** but **The Omen** had the real power.

The meadow filled with spring wildflowers had a warm spring at its west end. There was a legend about its healing powers. It could heal wounds. Some say it could even heal a man's soul. David had no interest in that part of the legend. He was impressed by the efficiency in which the group made camp. Moses had selected the best spot in the meadow for camp. Antonio and Moses unpacked the mules and let the horses out to graze on the tall green grass. Nick had built a firepit to start cooking. The others had gathered firewood for the night.

Their tents were arranged in the circle with the firepit in the center. Everyone had their own tent. Lo Ming had told everyone that they needed to be extremely careful in how they interacted with each other. David could use any weakness for his own gain. David must not know that some of them were more than just members of the group. He could use their relationships to split apart the group's cohesion.

Moses was not too happy with this arrangement. He wanted to be with Lo Ming. He had missed her. Lo Ming could see it in his eyes. She told him in his mind that it had to be this way. Moses caught a brief picture of her with his mother before Lo Ming could shut off that thought. Moses was curious about why she was thinking about his mother. Moses decided not to ask her about it. Maybe, Lo Ming was just thinking about the match they fought many years ago. He didn't think Lo Ming knew who his mother was.

Antonio tried to stay clear of being around Angela. He knew that David would be watching them closely. Angela had been David's bodyguard for many years. She was still acting that part. It didn't surprise him that she pitched her tent next to David's. Nick was somewhat relieved about the sleeping arrangements. He was caught in the middle between two people he loved. Shanna was his first love, and Rose was the person who had helped him with his problems on the first journey to The Land of the Eagle Feathers. He loved both for different reasons. He did notice that Rose seemed different toward him.

Nick could tell that Rose did not like Shanna being here. Nick did like how Shanna looked. She looked the part of a frontier woman in her brown leather outfit carrying that big Hawken 50 cal. rifle of John's. He would try to keep them from talking about him. If they knew about his relationship with each of them, that would be trouble.

Nick had the supper fixed in a short time. He had cooked a stew made from jerky and dried vegetables. He even had dessert made from fresh wild strawberries June had picked near the warm spring. Nick had not lost his touch. Everyone was always amazed that his food tasted so good. David had to admit that he was as good as any five-star chef that he had ever hired.

David told everyone after the meal that they would need to leave the horses here. June added, "I will contact Morning Star to come and get them." June stood up. Taking a golden hawk's feather from her pouch, she pointed to the sky and waved it. Soon a golden hawk flew down on to her outstretched arm. She whispered something to the hawk, and it flew away to the west. It made a grand sight against the red sunset as it flew. "Morning Star will be here tomorrow for the horses and mules and the supplies that we will need to leave behind."

Rose, being half Voodoo Priestess and half Cajun Wizard, sensed that Mary was having an extremely hard time with all of this. Mary had had her world turned completely upside down. It was only yesterday when she found out that she had a son somewhere. No matter how hard Mary tried to remember, she could not remember a thing about it. She knew that her father had accidently shot her. She had been in a coma for almost a year because of that incident. When she woke up, she had been told the baby had died in childbirth. The strange thing was that she remembered nothing about what had happened the previous two years. She didn't even know who the father was. These things kept circling are around in Mary's mind. She knew that her father probably knew more than he ever told her. Mary excused herself and went straight to her tent. She had to be alone. Lo Ming followed her.

Lo Ming caught Mary just as she got to her tent. "We are very worried about you. There is a warm hot spring at the end of the meadow that could help you relax and refresh. It is said that it can heal both physical and spiritual wounds. I will escort you there. A good bath and some time alone will do your soul good," Lo Ming said. Mary replied, "I don't want to do anything but to be alone." Lo Ming replied back, "This is not a request. You will go. We need you." Mary looked at Lo Ming. Mary knew that Lo Ming was right. Out here, everyone would need each other to survive. She had to get her head straight.

Rose took a cup with some water and put in some herbs and medicine she had brought. Placing the tin cup on the campfire, it was soon boiling. She was making a potion that her mother had taught her long ago. Mary would need it tonight. Rose knew it would be a long night for both her and Mary.

The rest of the group sat on logs or large rocks around the campfire. David told them that someone should be on watch. June replied, "Don't worry about that, I have it covered. My wolf, Midnight, will be watching and roaming the forest tonight. David smiled, "Whose wolf is the white one that I have been seeing?" "Oh, that is Snow, he belongs to One Feather," replied June. June was surprised that anyone could detect that Snow was around.

It wasn't long before Lo Ming and Mary came back from the warm spring. Lo Ming joined everyone near the campfire. Mary had gone straight to her tent. Rose took her tin cup and went to Mary's tent. When Rose got there, she asked Mary if she could come in. Mary replied, "Go away, I want to be alone." Rose replied back, "I know you don't. I have some medicine that will make you sleep. I will stay with you tonight. You will need me." Mary nodded her head. Mary knew better than say no. The last trip had taught her that Rose was very skilled in helping people with mental and spiritual problems. Mary realized that she needed all the help she could get, or she would go out of her mind.

Rose came into Mary's tent. She handed Mary her cup. Mary didn't say anything as she drank it down. Mary got dressed for bed and laid down. Soon she was fast asleep. Rose left. Rose would come back in about three hours. It would take that long for the potion to work.

Lo Ming had told the group that the warm spring was very relaxing. She suggested to them that they should take advantage of the spring. Angela laughed and said teasingly to Antonio, "I don't have a swimsuit." Antonio couldn't help but reply, "That never stopped you before." The others laughed at her comment. Antonio quickly realized that he had said too much. The others now knew that Angela and Antonio had a past. To keep it on a positive note, Antonio said, "That's the best invitation I had today. Let's all go. It will be fun."

It wasn't long before everyone had arrived at the warm spring. June and David had stayed back to watch the camp and the campfire. Also, Rose remained to watch over Mary. Nick wanted to stay back. Rose told him he needed to go with the others. Rose had sensed that something was wrong with Nick. He hadn't been the same since he had returned. Maybe it was that Shanna was here. Rose didn't think that that was it. It was something else. Rose hoped it was not what she suspected.

The warm pool was like one of the best spas in the world. Lo Ming took Moses by the hand and led him into the warm water. Her mind told him that she still loved him. They had to be careful with Angela, David and Shanna around. He told her back with his mind that he understood. Moses decided that he could have some fun by dunking Lo Ming into the pool. He picked Lo Ming up and threw her into the middle of the pool. He then jumped in beside her. They splashed and played like two kids. Nick couldn't keep his eyes off Shanna. She had only on her t-shirt and panties. They had become see thru the moment they had touched the water. Shanna enjoyed the way Nick looked at her. Antonio couldn't help it. He looked at Shanna too. Angela, not to be outdone, didn't even bother to wear that much. She splashed water into Antonio's eyes. When Antonio's eyes cleared, all he saw was Angela in all her glory. He quickly got her message. Antonio had better only pay attention to Angela. It would be very dangerous if he didn't. Angela grabbed him under the water in a very sensitive place to remind him that she wouldn't hesitate to cut it off.

After about an hour, they all arrived back at camp. June had fixed everyone some tea. The stars were out sparkling in the dark sky. Several shooting stars lit up the sky as their light traced their flight across the milky way. Everyone had a seat around the campfire. The warm fire felt good in the cool night's air.

The still night was soon broken by the howling of two wolves. As one stopped, the other answered. Antonio asked Moses what were they saying? Moses replied, "They are singing their love song to each other. It appears they missed each other over

13

the spring months. You can tell by the excitement in their voices."

Antonio couldn't help to ask, "Why do they howl at the moon?" June answered, "There is an Indian legend that explains that. The legend says that the moon once had a lover of the moon in the spirit world whose name was Quae Carca Jou. They fell in love. He would ride the wind until he was high enough to walk the skies with her. Every spirit in the spirit world knew of their great love for each other.

The other spirits were jealous of their great love. The most jealous spirit was called "Trickster." He wanted the moon for himself. Trickster developed a plan to separate Quae Carca Jou from his love, the moon. Trickster knew "Quae Carca Jou" would do anything to please his love. One day, Trickster told Quae Carca Jou that he heard the moon wanted some roses from the normal world, not ones from the spirit world. She thought the earth had the prettiest flowers. After all, she had seen them for years on her journeys around the earth. Quae Carca Jou decided that he must leave the spirit world to get the roses for his love. Trickster knew that Quae Carca Jou did not know that if he left the spirit world, he could not return to the spirit world. He would be trapped on earth.

When Quae Carca Jou came back with the roses, he could not get back into the spirit world. Try as he did, he could not go back. He soon realized that he could not walk the skies with the moon again. He would be trapped to spend his life on earth. On earth, Quae Carca Jou found a tribe that loved and worshiped the moon. He would look at his love, the moon, every night. He asked the Wolf Tribe to turn him into a wolf. He thought that he could help them. He knew that the Wolf Tribe had been harshly treated by others. He helped the Wolf Tribe. He was a brave warrior. The Wolf Tribe respected Quae Carca Jou's love of the moon. In turn for his assistance, they told him that they would let the moon know of his love. To do

14

this, they would have the wolves howl at the moon every night with him to tell her of his love. From that day forth, Quae Carca Jou and his fellow wolves go to the cliff tops every night and howl her name to let the moon know that Quae Carca Jou will always love her."

After a few moments of silence, Nick pointed to the moon. He asked, "Why do I see faces in the moon, especially that one that looks like a woman?" Lo Ming replied, "My Chinese ancestors have a legend about that face in the moon. My father once told me a legend about the faces in the moon when I was a little girl. Many people see faces in the moon. We have heard about the man in the moon, but many do not know about the woman in the moon. The woman is the Chang'e Woman who lives on the moon.

Long ago, there were mortal and immortal beings on earth. Two such immortal beings were the Chang'e Woman and her husband. They were not the best couple in the world. They were bad and did many bad things. They were very greedy. The spirits and gods did not like what they saw. They told them to change their behavior or receive punishment from them. The Chang'e Woman and her husband did not change. As punishment for their bad behavior, they were made mortal. The couple did not like being mortal. The Chang'e Woman did not want to grow old and ugly. They wanted to become immortal again. They would do anything to become immortal.

One day, they found a great priest. He told them that he had magical pills that could make them immortal. They would have to change their ways, especially their greed. The only problem was there was danger in taking the pills if they did not follow his instructions.

They did not. It appears that the Chang'e Woman got greedy and took too many of the pills in a hurry to become immortal. Her husband did not. Her greed caused her great harm. She ended up floating up to the moon where she remains, stuck forever. When you see the female face in the moon, it is the Chang'e Woman. The punishment for her was she would not get to enjoy being on earth ever again. Also, she would not have the company of her husband. Her husband pleaded to the gods and spirits to let him go to be with her. They replied. "No." They saw that he truly loved her. They told him that they would send her a rabbit to keep her company. That is why the shadows in the moon change sometimes. It is the woman playing with the rabbit."

It was starting to get late. Everyone went to their tent to get some sleep. Rose headed to Mary's tent. She knew it was going to be a long night. Hopefully, the potion would restore some of Mary's memory. If it did not, someone had put a very powerful spell on her.

I was just regaining consciousness when I heard two of the Unspeakables talking. "We have brought John here to our land to see what we should do with him. Should we let him try to obtain the other books of The Land of the Eagle Feathers?" I recognized the spirit's voice. It was Molden, the High Priest. He was talking to the Council of Spirits. I pretended to still be asleep. I would listen to them. I knew that sooner or later the Unspeakables would come for me. Their land was next to The Land of the Eagle Feathers. They had an interest in what I was doing. They knew that the Elders of The Land of the Eagle Feathers were growing weaker. The Unspeakables were afraid if someone or group got control of The Land of the Eagle Feathers, their land would fall next.

Margo, the Grand Priestess, replied, "I don't know about John. How do we know if he will keep his word? How do we know if he will not keep the books for himself? *The Book of Winter* contains too much power. We know that he has done the impossible by obtaining *The Book of Spring*. Nobody had ever done that before in all the hundreds of years that it had been hidden."

"You are right, Margo. The years have changed John. Now that he is half-ghost and half-man, he needs the books to have the power to save himself. I don't trust him. He leads a group that is very powerful. They are coming to rescue him. They are being led by a very evil person named David. He came here once many years ago. Why John chose to do this is what we need to know? Wake John up, we need to find out," stated Molden to the Council of Spirits.

"There is no need for that. I am awake," as I slowly stood up to face the Council. "I know that you have the power to destroy me. I know that you have always questioned my motives. I needed to show you that you need me. The Land of the Eagle Feathers and your land have been at truce for many centuries. We both signed The Treaty of the Eagle Feathers many years ago. I knew that once I obtained *The Book of Spring*, you would come for me. You have two things to be afraid of: someone like **The Dark Ones led by The Omen** finally gaining control of The Land of the Eagle Feathers and someone obtaining The Sacred Books of The Land of the Eagle Feathers. The second reason is more important to you. The books would make The Land of the Eagle Feathers more powerful than you or should I say: I more powerful than you."

Margo replied, "You are very wise. Why should we trust you? I know the answer. We have no choice. Your capture was part of your plan. You had the Old man and his dog contact us. You knew that we could not resist to capture you. You wanted to be here to tell us in person that you can do things that were once thought impossible.

You have one chance to survive. If the group you lead saves you, we will allow you to complete your quest. You were very cunning to have David lead your group here. He is the only one that has ever escaped from our land. Take John back to his cell. We will wait to see if you are worthy to finish your quest. Remember, John, we still don't trust you. Do not go back on your word. It would have dire consequences for everyone you love."

Rose checked on how Mary was doing. She found her fast asleep. Rose took her sleeping bag from her tent and laid down next to Mary. In about an hour, Mary started to talk in her sleep. It appeared that Mary was having a dream. Mary started talking about her father. She was saying something about being in love. It seems her father did not approve of Mary's choice of boyfriends. She was arguing with him. Her talking became almost impossible to make sense out of. There were bits and pieces of things. Mary started to tremble. Her dreams became nightmares. Rose held her close to try to comfort her. Later, Mary became quiet and fell into a deep sleep.

Up on the pass that had been closed due to the rockslide, the old man and his dog sat on a large boulder. "Well, I guess if we blow up this big one it should cause a slide and clear the pass. Most of the rocks should fall into the valley below. Hope there isn't anyone down below," said the old man to his dog. "I want you to go down to the trail and take this note I wrote and give it to Morning Star. I will set the charges and blow this pass open in about three hours."

The ground shook and immediately three loud explosions roared down to the valley below. Everyone jumped out of their tents to see what have happened. They could hear rocks and boulders falling down the mountainside. Moses told everyone not to worry. The rockslide would not reach them. "It was dynamite with three charges close together. By the sound of the rockslide and the explosions, I would guess it was at the pass that the slide closed yesterday. I have used dynamite in my mining operations in Australia. I know the sound," stated Moses to the others.

Moses told everyone to try and get some sleep. It would be three more hours before sunlight. They couldn't do anything until daylight. Rose went back to Mary's tent. Mary was still in a deep sleep. Rose put her arms around her and fell fast asleep.

It was getting first light when Nick started fixing breakfast. The smell of the food had everyone up. It would be another hour before the mist would clear to see the mountain clearly. Antonio watched as David was talking to Angela. They were off to the side of the camp. The sound of the nearby mountain stream covered up their conversation. Antonio, besides being a great language interpreter, could read lips. It wasn't hard for Antonio to decipher most of their conversation. It appeared that David was telling Angela to keep a close watch on Antonio. They couldn't afford for anything to happen to him. David told her to stay as close as possible to him. She would have to protect Antonio. Angela told him that she would do anything necessary. Antonio could see David laugh. David told her that he knew she would. This was good news to Antonio. He would definitely help Angela stay close to him,

It was about two hours later that Morning Star rode into camp. She had a note that she handed to June. Everyone gathered around while June read it out loud. "The pass is open. You can take the trail back up the mountain. You have no time to waste." David asked Morning Star, "Who gave that note to you?" Morning Star smiled, "An old hound dog."

Mary seemed to be in a better mood as she ate breakfast. Rose asked her if she remembered anything from her sleep. Mary replied that she remembered nothing except a woman's voice telling her it would take time to heal. Mary thought the voice was her mother's. That was enough for her. She had felt a calmness from that message. She would wait for her memory to come back to her.

Rose was worried. Someone had put a very powerful spell on Mary. If the potion didn't restore Mary's memory, then whoever did this to Mary was indeed very skilled. Mary did have a very powerful enemy.

Morning Star unpacked her lead mule. She opened several crates. Each crate had the weapons that John had given them in their first trip to The Land of the Eagle Feathers. John had told her to give them the weapons at the first sign of danger. David was not too surprised to see what each member of this group would be carrying. Mary had her bow and arrows. Rose had been given two bags of beads. June was given four golden hawk feathers. Shanna was given a leather vest full of throwing knives. Antonio was given a black, white tipped wand. Much to the surprise of David, he was given a gold coin. David didn't have to guess about what that was for. It appeared that John had thought of everything.

The others already had theirs. Lo Ming had her fighting stick, and Moses had his whip and large bowie knife already. David wondered why Nick didn't get anything. "Don't worry, I have my frying pan," Nick laughed, and the others laughed with him.

They made good time up the mountain trail. David was in the lead. Morning Star was the last one in line with the pack mules. They reached the pass about mid-afternoon. David halted the group. He sent Moses to look over the pass to see if it was safe.

Moses had been a miner. He was knowledgeable about explosives. He thought he was good with them. Whoever did this was an expert. They had to be very skilled at setting charges at the right depth with the correct amount of explosive. As he carefully walked through the pass, he checked both sides of the mountain pass for loose rocks. He whistled for David to bring the group through. Someday, Moses thought, "I want to meet whoever could do this." He marveled at the skill it took. Not only the blasts had to clear debris, it had to land where it could slide down the mountainside.

David led the others through the pass. It was a difficult stretch. You couldn't be calm. Another mountain slide could come. Everyone watched as they moved. Finally, they got through the pass. David told everyone that about three miles up the trail was a good place for a camp. There was a meadow for the horses to graze and good water. This indicated to everyone that David knew the terrain very well. He had been up here more than once.

They entered a cool mountain forest. The green pines carried a sweet refreshing scent. There were fewer hardwood trees this high up the mountain range. The air was warm with a late spring breeze. It took about four hours to reach the meadow. It would be dark in three hours. They quickly made camp. Nick picked some berries for dessert. June caught several trout in the mountain stream. It would be a good meal tonight. David did notice one thing about this mountain. There were many warm springs on this trail. It could only mean one thing. This mountain was once a volcano.

After their evening meal, Nick looked stressed. There were beads of sweat on his forehead. Rose asked him what was wrong. Nick told everyone that he could sense that they were not alone. About three clicks or two miles from here is a group following them. They are not friendly. David replied, "I sensed them an hour ago. Everyone will have to take a watch tonight. June will need to put out her wolf. Her friend has already put out his white one." Antonio said he would take the last watch. Angela volunteered for the one before it. The rest drew cards for the other times.

Nick drew the first watch. He didn't worry too much. The wolves were howling. That meant they had not detected anyone. It was when they stopped that they should worry. Shanna had the second watch. She relieved Nick. Nick had chosen a large boulder that overlooked the camp and much of the meadow. She was excited to get the chance to see Nick alone.

Nick was amazed that Shanna could be so silent. He did not realize she was behind him until she was about 20 feet away. Maybe it was the sound of the wolves that had distracted him.

21

Nick knew better. It was the pills that he had been taking to calm his nerves. Shanna was beautiful in the moonlight. Her dark auburn hair was loose down her back. She had that look of a lion hunting its prey. She had on tight shorts and a loose blouse. She carried her vest in her left hand. "Don't worry, Nick. I checked the perimeter. There is nobody out there for at least two miles," she said with a wicked smile.

She couldn't help herself. She grabbed Nick and planted a kiss on his lips. Nick pushed her away. Shanna wasn't surprised by his actions. She told him that she had noticed that Rose was interested in him. "Is Rose your new girlfriend?" Shanna teased him. Nick didn't answer her back. "Your silence speaks volumes. Don't worry. I won't make trouble for you. However, I did notice that Rose seems a little distant to you. Maybe, she has an old boyfriend somewhere. You two don't seem to be talking much." Nick didn't reply. He took his frying pan and left. Shanna thought, "I must be getting to the boy. I knew something is upsetting Rose. It is not me. I can wait. They will have to sort this out. I hope you can control your PTSD. It appears that you are having trouble. I will keep watch on you. It is only a matter of time."

June had the next watch. She wondered when One Feather would meet with her. She was lonely for his touch. She could go look for him after Moses took over for her. She had a plan to get his attention. Her watch was quiet with no sign of anyone approaching. Moses arrived to take over as planned. He told her to be careful on her way back to camp. June nodded. She had other things on her mind.

She headed down to the hot pool of the spring. Taking off her clothes, she walked slowly into the hot water, enjoying the water's heat. The water caressed each curve of her strong young body. She just floated in it. This must be what it would be like if you float in the sky on a cloud.

Being watched didn't bother her. She knew who was watching her. By the old cedar tree at the edge of the dark forest, he was there. She had noticed her admirer. That was why she decided to come here to bathe tonight. She could feel his eyes gazing at her body which made these moments even more exotic and exciting to her. Her skin tingled with anticipation. Would he come to her as he had in her dreams during the last few weeks? In the distance, their wolves were howling at each other.

Suddenly, she knew that she had made a mistake. Behind her, she heard a low growling sound. She instantly knew she was in trouble. It was the growl of a large cat. Then more growling followed from other large cats. It was a pack. She decided that they would probably not attack her in the hot pool of water. She very carefully stood up. What she saw wasn't good. There were four large black mountain lions at the edge of the pool. Their mouths were watering looking at her with their bright red eyes glowing following her every move. These panthers were not friendly. They were killers. A little hot water wouldn't stop them. If there was only one of them, her powers and strength would probably be enough to stop them. Four would be too much. She was trapped with little time to think. Her only hope was One Feather. She hoped that he would see her dire situation. She raised her arms to the night sky and sang the song of fire. The pool caught on fire around its edges. This would stop them for a few moments. Leaping out of the pool, over the fire she ran. It would be her only chance. It would a slim one at best.

The panthers caught her scent. They were quickly after her. It was only two hundred yards to the camp. It seemed like a hundred miles. They were closing in around her as she yelled for help. The leader of the pack jumped over her. Now in front of her, she was forced to stop. She was surrounded now. There was no hope. Their power would be too great to stop. Someone had sent them. Their glowing red eyes told her that.

Someone wanted her dead. It looked like that someone was getting their wish.

The large black leader growled at her. She would fight him. They would not have an easy time with her. The black leader pounced at her. She braced herself for him. Halfway in his leap, he stopped in mid-air falling to the ground in front of her. An Indian lance had stuck the cat's body. A white wolf appeared growling at the other panthers. The black leader had disappeared in a cloud of smoke. When her black wolf, Midnight, appeared, the other panthers disappeared into a cloud of smoke. Appearing out of nowhere, One Feather ran toward her. He grabbed her into his strong arms holding her tightly to his warm body. She was holding tightly to him in return as she fainted in his arms.

They had run from the camp toward June's yell as fast as they could. David caught a glimpse of the Indian brave holding June in his arms. One Feather quickly laid her down, grabbed his lance and disappeared into the night with his white wolf. Lo Ming arrived. She took off her jacket and covered June with it. Mary checked out June's condition. Mary found out why June fainted. In her arm was a small dart. It must have contained some type of drug. One Feather and the wolves had arrived in time. If June would have passed out before they arrived, the panthers would have had an easy time of killing her. Mary asked Nick to go back to her tent and bring her medical bag back as she attended to June. Antonio and Rose had stayed back at the camp to guard it.

David looked at the scene of the attack. There were footprints. The shoes were Native American. They were probably a man's. It was too large to be female. He followed the tracks for a few feet. The footprints disappeared. One thing that made the footprints different. They had a half moon imprinted on them. June had an enemy. David had once fought such a man. He was a great Indian Medicine Man. He was both powerful and cunning. He knew the way of the spirits. He would be extremely hard to beat. This Medicine Man did not have a tribe. He had been kicked out of several. David was learning quickly that this was not going to be easy. There were too many enemies out after what they wanted. There was one thing that he was going to do. June would get an ear full about being out here alone.

When David got back to camp, he ordered Angela and Antonio to relieve Moses. David knew that the danger was over for tonight. He wanted Angela and Antonio to renew their relationship. This would give him an ace in the hole. He could watch their moves better if they were entangled in a relationship. Relationships always come at a cost. June was proof of that tonight. Her relationship to One Feather almost cost her dearly. Also, it would give Moses a chance to see Lo Ming. He wickedly smiled. How could they not think he could feel the heat between them? They were easy to see through. It was another manner that he thought a relationship could cost them all. It was the triangle between Nick, Rose and Shanna. This could blow up in all their faces.

Angela was pleased to hear David's orders. Antonio knew what David's plan was. He would be glad to play along. That didn't mean he trusted Angela. Nobody that ever did trust her stayed alive long. He, like David, liked to play with fire. David's wife, Benita, was much like Angela, but deadlier.

Angela went to her tent to change. She covered herself with a blanket. She told Antonio that she was a little cold. The mountain air at night was colder. Little did Antonio know that Angela was naked under the blanket. She had other things on her mind. David told her that the danger had passed. It didn't take a genius to know what David meant. This was one order that she would make sure she followed.

Moses was happy that Angela and Antonio relieved him. He wanted to get back to try to see Lo Ming. Antonio filled in

Moses as to what had happened to June. Moses told Antonio he would have a talk with June. Angela told him David would take care of that. He should stay out of it.

After Moses left, Angela started to gather fresh grass and flowers from the meadow. She fashioned a nice soft cushion on the hard ground. She motioned for Antonio to join her. Antonio said that we should be on watch. Angela told him that David thought everything was safe for the rest of the night. David would be up anyway. He did not sleep much more than a few hours a night. It didn't take Antonio long to change his mind when Angela dropped her blanket on the cushion she had made. Her nude body was all the argument that was needed for Antonio to follow.

She whispered in his ear that she missed him so much. As he held out his hand to touch her, she pulled him down onto the blanket. Her long silky hair was soft to his touch. She kissed him longingly on his lips. Her kisses were always something special. Each one of her kisses more erotic than the other. Her warm supple body felt so smooth and inviting against his. He had missed their lovemaking. She was a vixen. Her hand slowly inched its way down his body to hold him. At the same time, his hand moved teasingly down her body.

He pulled her body close by gently grabbing hold of the cheeks of her perfect buttocks squeezing each of them, playing a game of alternating gentleness and roughness. He very slowly moved his hands to touch her most secret parts. He lowered his head to kiss her soft breasts. He took his time with his tongue encircling one hard nipple. He moved his head to be under each breast. She felt the light kisses as he licked the smooth softness under each. Angela could feel the heat of his kisses. His day-old beard added a different dimension of eroticism like day is to night.

His fingers told him that she was responding to his touch. The wetness of her sex was starting to flow, warming his fingers as he touched her delicate center. She cursed herself for she had lost control. She opened herself to him as he moved to be guided into her. He could feel the heat of her opening up to him like a lovely spring flower does during the first day of spring. They became one.

She was like an untamed wild creature as she felt his heat radiate to her very core. He moved so slowly. She raked his back with her long fingernails giving him both pain and pleasure. Her hips swaying faster and faster: drawing him deeper into her. His kisses became bolder and alternating from soft to love bites on her enlarged nipples. He kissed her savagely on her hot red lips. She returned the kisses biting his lips drawing blood. They moved together mating, panting like wild creatures of the night each taking what they wanted from each other. They were lost to a world of raw pagan lust until each of them were consumed by it. Their raw passion was building into one long continuous orgasm that made time stop. They both cried out loud in pure ecstasy more animal than human.

It was getting light as Antonio and Angela woke up. They would need to get back to the camp. When they got to their tents, they were already taken down. Everyone had eaten breakfast. Rose had put out some fresh clothes for Angela to change into. Angela went behind some thick bushes and changed quickly. Antonio could tell that everyone knew what they had been doing. He didn't care. Angela seemed to like the idea. David threw two breakfast bars at them. He told them that they had wasted enough of his time. Today, they would be climbing up the face of the mountain cliff ahead. Morning Star would be taking the animals back. By tomorrow morning, they would be starting their rescue of John if he were still alive.

Chapter II
To John's rescue:
What a high price to pay?

It had gotten light enough for them to start up the mountain trail. David was walking ahead of everyone. He was followed by Mary, Nick, Rose, Antonio, Angela, Shanna, Lo Ming and Moses. Moses decided that he should fall back and watch everyone. Besides. he was worried that someone could be following them.

He didn't trust David. He had heard of him in his travels around the world. People were afraid of him. He was known for his cruel and harsh ways of dealing with people. It was said of him that he had no moral compass. If you got in his way, he would likely kill you than to bargain with you. From personal experience, he knew that was true. Moses only hoped that they would survive this journey. If David didn't kill them, the Unspeakables could.

He had once had a run in with David many years ago. David had probably forgotten about the incident. Moses had been a young man. David would not recognize him as the man he was now. It was in Mongolia. Moses and his mother were looking for hidden treasure and artifacts that belonged to Genghis Khan. They were in the Gobi Desert. His mother believed that she was the great, great, granddaughter of the famous ruler.

It was just the two of them in the vast desert. There were sand dunes as far as the eye could see in any direction. Moses thought they were lost. His mother insisted that she knew where they were. "How could she?" he thought. She did not even use a compass to check the maps they carried. He asked his mother, "Why don't you use the maps that we had brought." She answered him, "Because the maps don't cover this place. Nobody goes here. We are the first people to cross here in over

two hundred years. It is said that to go here is to die here."
Moses just replied to her saying, "That's great to know."

The camels were pretty well spent when they arrived at the
other side of the dune that she had pointed out. Moses didn't
see any water or anything else. His mother told him to take the
shovel and dig. Moses thought she was crazy. He got off his
camel and took a shovel from the supply pack on the pack
camel. He started to dig. After about two meters down, water
started to fill the hole he had dug. He let the camels drink their
fill before his mother and him drank. That was the custom in
the desert. The animals came first. They are what you need to
survive.

His mother pointed toward a large square rock. "Go and push
on that rock," she commanded him. He did as his mother said.
He pushed on the rock with all his might. As he was about to
give up, the rock moved. Behind the rock was a sand dune that
started to melt away. Like magic, a golden building appeared.
A large gold door opened. They both entered the building. It
was pitch black inside. Moses lit a torch. His mother and him
discovered that they were entering a large treasure room. There
were gold coins, statues and jewels of all kinds on the floor
piled high in the center. Moses jumped up and down. They
were rich. His mother told him that they were not to take
anything. They had come for one thing only. It was a golden
staff of her great, great grandfather that she wanted. She
believed that it should be hers. It was supposed to have magical
powers. After looking for it, she found it. She told Moses that
they must leave everything else.

Quickly, they started to turn and leave the building. Standing
in the doorway was a man and several of his men. It was
David. David told his mother to give the gold staff to him or he
would have his men kill them. They pointed their guns at them.
His mother knew that they had no choice. She handed the staff
to David. David laughed at her, "You knew that I wanted the

staff. I told you that I would get it. I will let you live. All you need to do is get out of this desert on foot. I will take your camels. I hope you survive, but I doubt it.

Moses remembered watching David and his men leave them with only a few canteens of water. What David didn't know was that Moses was a man of the Outback. He knew how to survive in the desert. His mother looked at him. "I know we will survive. Your grandfather has taught you the secrets of the desert. We will survive!" That is what they did. They survived the desert. Later, Moses tracked down every man that David had with him. They didn't survive. He knew someday that he would meet David again. He would do nothing to him. He needed David to find John and save him. He also had promised his mother that David would be hers to do with as she wanted to. He was not the boy that David had left in the desert. There was only one big problem. David had saved his life. This meant that Moses had to abide by The Land of the Eagle Feathers rules.

Antonio was feeling very vulnerable. He didn't know if David knew that he had deciphered *The Book of Spring*. Antonio's instinct told him that David had set him up and had used him all along. That fact gave Antonio some satisfaction. If David knew, David would need to keep him alive until Antonio deciphered all the books. After that, Antonio hoped that Angela was really on his side. He would need her to survive. Besides, they had a plan for this land themselves.

Several members of the group were reflecting on the events of the past several days. Shanna had tried her best to fit in. She had recognized at once that Nick did not want to let on that he had known her before. She would need to explain her presence. Shanna made it clear that she was here only because John had hired her to protect him from David. She had told everyone that John had known her for several years. He had once saved her life in a war several years ago. She had done some work for him throughout the years. She mostly did it because she felt she owed it to him. She did note that he did pay her well.

Angela was in a different situation than Shanna. She was with David. Nobody in the group trusted her. She had kept quiet and to herself for most of the trip. She knew that once the group knew about her relationship with Antonio things were going to change. Members of the group would have a lot of questions for Antonio to answer. Would they trust Antonio because of their relationship? Both David and she needed for Antonio to obtain the rest of books. He was the only one that could decipher them. She believed that after they rescued John; David and her would need to go back and take Shanna with them. They would have to anyway. The Land of the Eagle Feathers wouldn't let David and Shanna have access to the land.

They reached the cliff after a few hours of hiking. On the side of the steep face of the cliff was a cave. It was about 60 feet straight up. David pointed to the cave. "We will have to get to that cave. The cave will take us to where they are holding John. We have enough rope to use to get to the cave. To make the climb easier, we will leave our packs here. Once everyone is up to the cave safety, we will pull up each of our packs one at a time. We will leave Angela here to attach the rope to each of them. She will be the last one to climb up to join us. I would leave Shanna back, but I would be tempted to cut her rope."

Shanna volunteered to be the first one up. She had training and a lot of experience in mountain climbing. Everyone watched as she cautiously climbed. She was a natural on the mountainside. She placed metal stakes for a rope about every ten feet. It wasn't long before she was at the cave opening. She tossed down another rope as a safety rope to attach to the other climbers in case they would lose their handholds. She would hold onto the safety rope and reel it in.

Everyone laughed when she told David that he should go next. "Don't worry, David. I won't cut your rope. At least not yet," she yelled down to him. David smiled and attached himself to the safety rope and started to climb. He easily made it up. It wasn't long before everyone completed the climb. Angela was the last one after she sent the packs up.

David told everyone to take a few minutes to rest. It would take them about four hours to get out of the cave. They had to be very silent in their movements. When they got to the end of the cave, they would arrive at the Land of the Unspeakables. He would motion for them to put out their flares before they arrived at the end of the cave. There may be someone waiting for them. They would have to know that somebody would be coming for John.

David lit up his flare. Nick whistled. On both sides of the cave's entrance were precious gems of all kinds. David told them to not bother any of the gems. They were put there for a reason. Anybody disturbing them would set off an alarm. Antonio thought that was a very interesting idea. He would try to restrain himself.

The travel through the cave was difficult. After about 4 hours, David held up his hand. They extinguished their flares. David asked June to join him at the front of the line. There was brush and tall grass blocking the exit from the cave. June took out one of her hawk feathers. Waving it three times in the air, a hawk appeared on her shoulder. David moved the brush and tall grass just enough for the hawk to fly out of the cave. June took out a clear crystal from her pouch. She looked down at the crystal. She could see in the crystal what the hawk was seeing.

The crystal revealed that nobody was around the exit to the cave. The land was beautiful. There were fields of grain and orchards of fruit trees. In the distance was an old castle. It had high walls and a moat around it. In the distance, the sky was dark. A thunderstorm was forming in the distance.

David told the others to leave everything in the cave including knives, bows and arrows, throwing knives and John's black powder gun. They would have to rely on their wits and cunning to do this job. If they got John out without anyone getting hurt, the Unspeakables would honor their skills. David asked June, "Did One Feather come?" June nodded.

David told everyone his plan. We will need to get into the castle. Rose will create a diversion. When it gets dark, she will set up several places with her exploding beads. At the stroke of 2 p.m., she will set them off one at a time. When the last set of beads explodes, Moses will blow the front drawbridge door to the castle. That will cause the drawbridge to go down, and the front entrance will be wide open. I have two sticks of dynamite for you to use. It seems that someone left these at the pass for me to find. It had a note on them saying, "These will open some special doors."

It is my estimation that the thunderstorm will hit us about 12 o'clock. We will have about 2 hours to scale the walls and find John. Antonio will use his wand to knock out the two guards near the back of the castle. That will give us a chance to scale the walls. June's hawks will carry this rope over the walls. One Feather will tie the rope to something solid for us to climb over. Antonio, you must time the wand's lighting with the lightning of the storm. Everyone, listen, do not kill or seriously hurt anyone. If you do anything like that, they will destroy us all. One Feather, being a spirit warrior, can only be here for a few short hours before he must return to the Land of the Eagle Feathers. We will leave for the castle at dusk. Get some rest, there will be none until we are safely back in this tunnel.

I had been pacing back and forth in my cell for several hours. I could hear the thunderstorm coming. Molden stopped in to see me. "I know what you are thinking, John. You think that tonight would be a great time to escape. The storm would be a great distraction. I don't think that tonight will be the night.

David doesn't like storms, especially heavy rain. Water takes some of his powers away. He will probably try tomorrow night instead. We have set up some plans for that. Oh! There is one more thing. We caught this golden hawk. It had a note for you. It says that we will see you at midnight tomorrow. It was at your window over there in the corner waiting for me to leave. I think you should have it as a pet. I will release it to you in your cell. It will remind you that your escape is futile. Have a good night's sleep, John," Molden stated as he walked out.

I gently picked up the hawk that June had sent me. Under its left wing was hidden a small bead. I told the hawk that he would have to become a small sparrow to escape and show the others where I was. I held the hawk up and said, "A sparrow for now you will be, but to save others you will not mind. Now fly to your master and sing your song. Then, you will become a mighty hawk once again." The hawk became a sparrow. I released the sparrow to fly through the steel bars of my cell. The sparrow flew out the open window. They would know where I was. Sometimes, a little bird is as good as a great eagle.

The storm hit at midnight. Rain came down in great white sheets. You could hear it hitting the roof. I figured about between one and two a.m. my escape would begin. At one, the door to the dungeon opened. Standing there wet as a duck, was David with June, Nick and Angela. I asked, "Where were the others?" David said, "Outside having fun."

I put the small bead into the lock. It exploded exactly at 2 a.m. I was free. David motioned for us to hurry. We would need to get out now. We ran down the two flights of stairs to the outside doors. Everyone was looking at the front large doors that had been blown down by Moses's dynamite. We climbed the ropes at the back walls. Rose was still lighting her beads taking her time exploding them one at a time. As we were about down the back side of the back wall, a guard yelled at us. Antonio took aim and knocked him down. We ran for the cave as fast as we could. Moses and Rose were already there. Lo Ming was guarding the cave's exit. We were all about back in the cave except for Shanna. David and Nick were just in front of her. She saw a flash coming from the castle. She jumped and knocked both of them down, but she got hit by part of it. David and Nick were safe. Shanna was not. She had a deep cut and some burns on her back. Nick grabbed Shanna and dragged her into the cave. He carried her to Mary. Mary had her medicine kit. She immediately started to give aide to Shanna. Moses told everyone to get behind the next turn in the wall. He blew the exit to the cave.

Nick started shouting and acting like a crazy man. He had had enough. Seeing Shanna hurt badly, and the number of explosions were too much. Nick was having a meltdown. Rose tried to calm him. That was having no effect. Lo Ming took her fighting stick and knocked him out with one blow. John and David looked at each other. David said, "That was too easy. I don't think I can trust you."

The Unspeakables were not happy with the turn of events. Molden was talking to Margo. Margo was not happy with John escaping so easily. "You had your chance to kill David, and you missed," said Margo. "If it hadn't been for that girl knocking him out of the way, I would have gotten David," Molden replied. "That was your game all along, wasn't it?" Margo asked. "Yes, it was. I must admit that John was very good in the part he played. He got David to come here. I just missed," Molden said reluctantly. "Are you so sure that you could trust John? He did give you the wrong night that they would rescue him. I'm not so sure, maybe he had other things that he wanted," Margo said, trying to make a point.

Molden looked at Margo. There is one thing that John would need to assist him in hunting the books. I better go check. Wait here for a few minutes while I check it out," Molden said in a hurry. Molden went to his room. He looked in the small trunk by his bed. It didn't take him long to notice that a special red gem was gone. Angerly, he went back to talk to Margo.

"You were right. One of his group must have used the escape to get into my room to get the special gem. John tricked me all along. He used his escape to cover the fact that one of his group could slip into my room and get the gem," Molden said. Margo laughed as she said, "John is still as smart as ever. He tricked you. Now, he has the Red Gem of Discovery. That should help him find the other books. He certainly set you up."

In the darkness of the cave, David looked at me. "Yes, I got what I wanted. One Feather took the Gem of Discovery from Molden's room. He gave it to me when nobody noticed. I have it in my pocket."

David replied, "I still got the impression that the fireball from Molden wasn't a friendly gesture. Molden still wants to kill me for several reasons."

"Yes, he does. You knew we needed the gem to find the books. You didn't do so bad for yourself. I did give you a rare golden Roman coin worth several hundreds or even a million for your help," I told him. David took out the gold coin he got from Morning Star and smiled. Mary told David to get out of her way. Shanna will need some help to get back. She is weak. She will need someone to assist her."

"Since she did save my life, I will have to do it. That is the rule," said David. "John, you will have to do something about Nick. We still need him to find the location of the other books."

Since Shanna was not hurt as bad as they originally thought, Mary turned her attentions to Nick. Mary noticed right away that Nick was sweating and shaking. She asked Lo Ming to help her take off Nick's shirt. As Lo Ming was unbuttoning Nick's shirt, two bottles of pills fell out on to the cave's floor. David said, "I thought so. He had the signs of popping pills. I have been watching him the last few days. What's his problem, John?" John looked at the others that had gathered around. "He's got PTSD. I had hoped that he was doing better. He did things in the war in the Middle East that he has not forgiven himself for. We need to get him back together as fast as we can. Does anyone have any ideas?" John replied.

Lo Ming said, "I know of a healing ceremony that could help him. Mary and Rose said it at the same time, "Reiki." Mary stated that we would need a Reiki Master to perform such a healing ceremony. Lo Ming said, "I am."

Mary told everyone that they would need to have a large enough space to do such a ceremony. David told her that he knew of a place in the cave that was a large room. He had discovered it when he was lost in the cave many years ago. Moses had found two poles to make a stretcher. Placing Nick in it, Moses and John picked it up and followed David. Antonio assisted Shanna with the others following. After about four hundred yards, David turned down a side tunnel. You could hear water. They made their way carefully. The path was rocky, barely wide enough for them to pass. After about 150 yards, they saw some light. When they made a right turn, they saw it. The light was coming from the top of the cave. A small stream of water from the outside was entering the cave above them. The room was large enough for everyone to sit. There wasn't much light, but enough to see each other. They placed Nick's stretcher in the center of the room.

Lo Ming told everyone that she would describe what was going to happen. "Long ago, I studied under Grand Master Mikao Usai in Japan. He was the first to promote the healing on a larger scale. It took me several years to become a Grand Master.

Reiki is a technique that involves palm healing. Reiki is divided into two words. Rei is light. Ki is energy. In Reiki, a universal energy is transferred through my palms to Nick in order to encourage emotional and physical healing. The life force energy will be guided by the higher intelligence over each chakra.

The Ki energies will flow out of my body while I am touching Nick. I will place my hands over the area of each chakra of Nick's body. It will be necessary to place my hands on each chakra for healing. You will see the following colors: Red for the root chakra, Orange for the sacral chakra, Yellow for the solar plexus chakra, Green for the heart chakra, Blue for the throat Chakra and Indigo for the brow or third eye chakra. Each person has the seven chakras, which are energy fields. When there is an imbalance of energy flow in any of the chakras, the person gets sick. The purpose of Reiki is to restore proper energy flow in the chakras.

There will be an emphasis on the color purple. That is the color of the Crown chakra, which is Nick's dominant chakra. When the flow of energy is balanced, you will see a white light. The white light is a combination of all the seven colors of the chakras. This will indicate that the energy flow is balanced, and the healing ceremony is successful. I will need ten minutes to meditate. We can only have positive thoughts when I perform this ceremony. I suggest that David go to another place while I perform this. David looked at everyone and said, "I think she is right. It is hard for me to think positive. I have too much going on to think otherwise."

Lo Ming told everyone that she will need to bring the energies from the four directions: North, East, South and West. Moses replied, "I will draw you a compass in the dirt of the cave. I know that it will be hard for you to tell where each direction is in this cave. I suggest that you go to the far end of this large room. The falling water from above into the pool will give the most solitude. Water falling will assist you in drawing the energy you will need. My grandfather taught me that in the Outback. I will place the four points of the compass in the

38

exact positions near the falling water. Please stay here until I am done. You will need all the energy that you can receive."

Moses headed toward the falling water at the end of the cave. He raised his hands. As if guided by an unknown force, he turned and marked each direction in the dirt by the pool. He said something in his native language from the Outback. We thought he must be thanking his ancestors for their guidance. He returned and sat down. His eyes were wide and full of spirit. Without saying anything, Lo Ming walked carefully over to where Moses had drawn his directions. The only sound in the cave was the water hitting the pool below it. Lo Ming felt the energy of the falling water. She raised her arms and pointed toward the falling water. After about five minutes, she moved her hands toward her as she gathered the energy into her body. She turned to each direction: East, South, West and finally North, performing the same movement to each direction. She felt full of the healing energies. The group had formed a circle around Nick's stretcher. They did not say anything when Lo Ming returned. They only stared at Nick. They would give her all the positive energy they could muster.

Lo Ming knelt beside Nick's body. She was in a deep trance. Taking her hands, she started at the lower parts of Nick's body. With her hands, palm down, she touched each chakra of his body.

You could see the color of each transfer from his body. First was Red for the root chakra. Orange flowed next for sacral chakra. Yellow followed for his solar plexus chakra. Green light flowed from his heart chakra. As she moved to his throat, a beautiful shade of Blue appeared. She moved to his brow or third eye chakra in which indigo lit up in her palms. Lo Ming, knowing that Nick's dominant chakra was his crown chakra, moved her hands very slowly toward it. As she approached his head, the room lit up into the color of Purple. This is where his energy was unbalanced. Lo Ming touched the top of his head and held her hand there. The group tried with all their energy to think positive thoughts. Lo Ming would need all her energy to transmit and balance this chakra. This took several minutes.

Rose and Mary watched very carefully. They concentrated their energies toward Lo Ming. The Purple sparkling light started to change. The dark purple seemed to slowly change its hue. It was getting lighter. The light from Lo Ming's palms was turning white. The large cave's room took on the glow of white. Lo Ming had done her work. A white light filled the room. Nick's chakras were in balance. It was done. Mary stood up. She announced to everyone, "It is finished."

Moses caught Lo Ming as she fainted. Lo Ming was spent. It would take her several hours to regain her strength. They would have to wait until Nick would regain consciousness to see the results.

I had left with David, Angela and Shanna before the ceremony had begun. I didn't want to take any chances on any negative thoughts during the ceremony. When I saw the White light, I told David to take Angela and Shanna back to the Eagle Train Station. I knew that David would take care of Shanna. Shanna had saved David's life.

The group looked up. I appeared from the side tunnel. Antonio asked where the others were. I told them that I had them return to the Eagle Train Station. They would assist Shanna back. Morning Star would be waiting with the horses below the cliff. They had to go back. They could not go with us to The Land of the Eagle Feathers. There is a side tunnel that would lead us to The Land of the Eagle Feathers. It is better to not have Nick see Shanna. He is just starting to heal from his past. She is part of his past. Antonio, you know my reasons for not having Angela here. Go get our packs and come back here. By the time you return, they should have recovered enough for us to resume our journey to obtain *The Book of Summer.*

Chapter III
The Council Meeting:
Is the Council behind them?

Antonio located the packs. He noticed that on the wall behind the packs was some ancient writings. This must be the other entrance to The Land of the Eagle Feathers. Examining the writings, he knew that someone with David's knowledge could probably decipher the language they were written in. He would confront John later. John had been holding out on him. There were two entrances to The Land of the Eagle Feathers. Why hadn't he told everyone? John must have a reason.

I saw Antonio coming back. He didn't have the packs with him. "Where are the packs? I asked him. Antonio stated back, "I found them where you had left them by the other entrance to The Land of the Eagle Feathers." I could see the mistrust in his eyes. The others had gathered around. "Yes, there is another entrance to The Land of the Eagle Feathers. I spent many years trying to find it. Many years ago, David and the Dark Ones found a way into The Land of the Eagle Feathers. The only way I could stop them was to gather a large group of warriors to fight them. Let's say that we did prevail, but at a great cost in life. Now that I have found the passage, we will make sure that nobody can use it again. After we get out of this part of the cave, I will have Moses blow the passage shut. Nobody will ever be able to use it again, against us," I replied back to Antonio and the group.

Rose looked at me. "John, we know there is much more to that story. Perhaps, you will tell us more someday." I replied back, "Yes, I will tell everything to you one day but not today. We must get out of here before the Unspeakables try to find us."

Lo Ming and Nick had recovered enough to travel. Antonio led everyone back to the packs. I found mine and gave two sticks of dynamite to Moses. He nodded back to me that he knew what to do with them. Everyone put on their pack. I told everyone to run as fast as they could after Antonio said the words on the wall. We would need to get clear of Moses' charges when he blows up the entrance.

Antonio started to read the writing, "We welcome you to The Land of the Eagle Feathers. We will only let you in if you destroy this passage. Only John and The Keepers of the Yawi are allowed to pass. We have been awaiting you for a long time. You must promise to destroy this passage to save the Land of the Eagle Feathers. Now go! May the spirits be with you." The wall opened. Everyone ran through the opening.

As we reached the end of the tunnel and saw the sunlight, we heard the mountain shake. Moses had set off one of the charges. We could only hope that he would make it back to us. Dust filled the tunnel as we cautiously ran to the daylight outside the tunnel. We turned and looked back at the cave's entrance. A dusty figure appeared. Lo Ming ran into his arms and kissed Moses passionately. Caught by surprise, Moses started to blush. "That is a nice picture. We must get moving. We have only two days to get to the mountain for the Council Meeting. One Feather will lead us there. He knows some shortcuts," I told them.

In the bright sunlight, Antonio got a good look at One Feather. There was something about him that seemed very familiar. As he looked in One Feather's eyes, he felt sometime different. For a brief moment, he saw Angela and himself. One Feather felt something when their eyes met. One Feather brushed off the feeling. He had more important things to do.

The Land of the Eagles Feathers' Council had seated themselves. There was much to discuss before John and his group arrived for the Council meeting. In two days, they would be arriving. Red Woman and the Great Elder wanted to have their Council's message to John and his group in accordance with the Council's wishes.

The Council meeting was being held in the Sacred Cave of the Eagle Mountain. The Great Elder had heard that one member of the Council had been very vocal about the mission of John's group. The Council of The Land of the Eagle Feathers consists of seven tribal members. Each member having been selected by the tribe for their great powers and courageous deeds. The Great Elder is the leader of the Council. The Red Woman is a member that is very powerful. She can decide many issues because of her position in the tribe. The Great Elder called the meeting of the Council to call out anyone that might cause problems.

Each member of the Council was seated cross-legged around the sacred fire in the middle of the Council Room. The Great Elder had decided to bring his Talking Stick to the meeting.

A Talking Stick would only allow one member to speak at a time. The one that brings their talking stick is known as a "tree." Great Elder's Talking Stick was made of Birch which means "tree of truth." It was decorated in the color Black which means clarity and focus. Accompanying the Talking Stick is a feather. This feather is called the answering feather. The answering feather symbolizes the meaning of the bird that the feather comes from. The Great Elder chose the bird feather of the Owl. The person that is asked a question by the member with the Talking Stick must answer the question with what the feather represents. The Owl feather represents stopping any deception by the member that answers the question from the member that gives the feather to that member.

The Great Elder rose from his seated position to start the Council Meeting. In his hands was his Talking Stick of Birch, decorated in the color of Black. It was easy to see that the Great Elder was upset.

The Great Elder looked at the members in front of him. He spoke to everyone there, especially Blackhawk. "I have called this Council Meeting to discuss some things I have heard. As you know, we are trying to obtain the four books of the seasons. John and his group, **The Keepers of the Yami,** have already obtained *The Book of Spring.* They have a slight chance of finding all the books. I understand that Blackhawk has some concerns about them obtaining all the books especially *The Book of Winter.* I want to hear his concerns. Here is my Talking Stick with the Owl Feather attached. The Great Elder went over to Blackhawk and gave it to him.

The Council Room became quiet. Blackhawk, being an older member of the Council, was held with much esteem. He stood up straight and tall. Taking the Talking Stick and the Owl Feather, he knew it was his sacred honor to give his Sacred Point of View in answering to the one that questioned him with a Talking Stick. Nobody is allowed to talk unless they hold the Talking Stick. Everyone must listen to the one that has the Talking Stick even if they disagree with them.

Blackhawk was not one to be called out in a Council Meeting. Sweat had formed on his forehead. He knew that he must tell everyone what he felt. "Yes, I have several concerns. If John obtains all the books, he will become enormously powerful. How do we know if we should trust him with such power? He does have reasons to turn his back on us. We have been very critical of him in the past. When he gave his life to protect this land, we only gave him half his life back. He has been very protective of us. He has spent many moons protecting us. I find that the Great Elder has not given him credit for his sacrifice. Why should we trust him, when we have treated him this way?" questioned Blackhawk to the Great Elder. Blackhawk was wise to give the Talking Stick back to the Great Elder with the Owl Feather. It was easy for Blackhawk to turn this around. Now, everyone has their eyes on the Great Elder. It was his time to answer.

"Yes, I know your concerns. Maybe, I have been hard on John. You sometimes must heat the wood to make it bend to make a bow. That does not mean that the bow does not shoot its arrow straight and true. John protects us because this is the only place that he can call home. I understand your concerns. That is why I have something that John has always wanted: a son," stated the Great Elder. The Great Elder handed the Talking Stick and the answering feather to the Red Woman. "The Red Woman knows what I say is true."

The Red woman began to speak, "For several years, I have taken in a boy. He is my grandson. You all know him. He is the son of John. John knows that he has a son, but he does not know who he is. I told him that before he was captured by the Unspeakables. Don't get me wrong. John will be very hard to deal with when he comes back for the Council meeting on Eagle Mountain. I will watch him very carefully. John is a very clever man. I worry about him. He once saved my life. I am wise enough to know that John will only take power if he needs it. Do I trust him? The answer to that is maybe. Does he trust the Great Elder and me? The answer to that is No! That is why we have the advantage with him," replied the Red Woman to the Great Elder.

The Red Woman handed the Talking Stick back to the Great Elder. The Great Elder spoke his words very carefully, "No matter what, we must remember that those who have one foot in the canoe and one on the ground are going to fall into the river. The wise man, Tuscharara, spoke those words. We cannot fall in the river. We must move forward upstream or the river will overtake us. John is like the frog. The frog must not drink up the pond in which he lives."

Blackhawk nodded his head in agreement. "I see it clearly. I ask the Council to vote on supporting John's mission." The

Great Elder put it to a Council vote. They all voted to support John and his group.

We had only a couple of days to get to the Council Meeting on top of the Sacred Eagle Mountain. One Feather had joined us as we had emerged from the tunnel. I told him to take us the shortest way to the mountain meeting. Time is a circular dimension. In this region, it moves fast and slow. I asked One Feather what day it was. He laughed. He said, "We have three days to make our Council meeting. We would have to travel most of the day and night before we could stop to get there in time.

Mary and Nick seemed to be recovering well. Mary was not as subdued. She was talking more to Rose and Lo Ming. Nick was strong physically. I would watch to see if he was doing better mentally. I had seen PTSD. It would take some time for him to heal. Lo Ming had done an excellent job with him. I told everyone that the next two days would be very difficult. We would have to push ourselves to make the deadline for the meeting.

The bright morning sunlight felt warm on our bodies. It was good to leave the damp cold cave. I never get tired of looking at the beauty of The Land of the Eagle Feathers. Below us was a green valley surrounded by high mountain peaks. One Feather pointed to a distant white mountain. "That is where we are going. We will have to travel fast with few breaks. I will lead," he said.

Behind One Feather, I put June followed by: Nick, Lo Ming, Mary, Rose, Moses and Antonio. I wanted to have Antonio in front of me. He's a scorpion. You must always watch a scorpion.

The trail took us down into the rich green valley. There was wildlife in abundance by the small streams and meadows filled with wildflowers blooming in the warm sun. It didn't take long for us to peel off our warm jackets and shirts. You could tell that summer was arriving. After about three hours, One Feather called a halt by a mountain stream. There were a couple of large Oak trees which gave us some shade from the hot sun. He told everyone to drink their fill and to fill their canteens. The water here was pure. It had special properties that would give us more strength. We would need it for the march ahead of us. Nick gave out to everyone some energy bars he had made.

June had seated herself near One Feather on a boulder near the rushing stream. They looked at each other more than talked. I noticed Antonio watching and studying One Feather. It was like Antonio was trying to figure out something about One Feather. I smiled to myself. Perhaps, one day he would figure out why he was drawn to One Feather. When he did, that day would be very difficult for both of us. I didn't worry about Antonio too much. It would be Angela that would probably try to kill me. She had already tried it once.

Mary was talking to Rose and Lo Ming. I could see in her eyes that she was returning to a more normal state of mind. I could sense that it was difficult for the others to believe that Mary could be a threat to anyone. Mary had told them that her father and her were not close at all. I could tell that Antonio did not believe her. The others seemed to take her word at face value.

Moses picked up a rattlesnake near him. He seemed to be talking to the snake. Moses laughed. He put the large snake down in front of the trail ahead of us. Nick asked him why he did that. "The rattlesnake is inviting me to a snake dance. It is an honor for us to attend," Moses replied. Nick just shook his head. Antonio muttered something like, "That will be the day."

We soon started up the trail. It felt good to enter the thick green forest. The dark forest did not allow much sunlight. Moss was growing on some of the large flat rocks on the trail. We were making good time. Moses noted that everyone must have stayed in good shape over the spring. Sweat was starting to run down their T-shirts. At this rate, we would be stopping about midnight at a good place to camp. It had a nice cool spring in the meadow. A good dip in that pool would soon make us forget about the long hot hike today.

Angela and David had taken their time to return back to the bottom of the cliff. They had lowered Shanna down the rockface of the cliff very closely. Angela didn't like the turn of events. She wanted to follow John's group into The Land of the Eagle Feathers. With David here, she could not do that. If David had ever found out that she could, her job and life would cease to exist.

Shanna had been apprehensive about leaving with David and Angela. She was worried about her safety. David reassured her that she had little to fear. He would honor his commitment to not hurt anyone that had saved his life. David did ask a lot of questions to Shanna. Shanna would only give short answers that were vague. David knew that Shanna knew more than she was willing to give him.

Morning Star was waiting for them at the base of the cliff. David asked her, "How did she know to be there? She smiled and answered, "The old hound dog told me to come." Shanna was feeling much better. Her wounds were healing quickly. Morning Star told her that they would be stopping to camp at a healing pool tonight. This pool would assist Shanna in healing her burns. She would not have any permanent marks from the burns on her skin.

A sudden thunderstorm hit us about five o'clock. This was no surprise this time of year. The rain came down in sheets. It wasn't long before everyone was wet to the bone. It was nice to be clean from the rain. Our clothes were wet and clung to our bodies. Most of us stripped off our shirts and hung them on the backs of our packs to dry. Most of the women just put on short tops. They had prepared for this type of weather. The footing on the trail had become slippery. This slowed us down. It was about 1 a.m. when we stopped for the night to pitch camp.

It wasn't long before the camp was set up. Nick had a fire started in a few minutes. Moses had found some branches to use for us to put our wet clothes on to dry by the fire. I told Nick that his grandfather had taught him well in using his fire-starting talents. Nick knew what I meant. I had witnessed him using a ball of flame between his hands to start the wet wood.

Rose was worried about Nick. She told him if he wanted to, he could put his tent together with hers. She told him she was still worried about him and the side-effects of the ceremony that Lo Ming had performed. Nick was a little hesitant but agreed with her. He didn't want to be alone. He knew that Rose could control his anxiety. That was great comfort for him.

Nick fixed the meal of stewed jerky and wild rice with cornbread. Mary had picked some blackberries along the way for dessert. After the meal, Nick asked if anyone knew the Native Indian legend about summer and winter. Nick said his Grandfather had told him about it once, but Nick had forgotten how it went. June said she did know of a story about summer fighting winter. Several of the others encouraged June to tell the story.

June said this is how it goes---

There was an Aroma chief who had a daughter named Co-Chin. She was married to the Spirit of Winter, Shakok. She was very unhappy in her marriage because it was arranged for her by her father. The land she lived in was barren. No crops would grow after she married Shakok.

One day, Co-Chin was gathering cactus leaves. While she was cleaning off the thorns of the cactus leaves, she met a young man. In the young man's hand, he carried an ear of green corn. Co-Chin asked the young man where did he get the corn? The young man gave Co-Chin the ear of corn and told her that tomorrow he would bring her more from his home in the South.

The next day the young man brought Co-Chin a whole bundle of corn. Co-Chin told him that she wanted to go see his home in the South. It must be a lovely land to have so much corn. The young man told Co-Chin that "Your husband, Shakok will get angry if you do.

Co-Chin said, "I do not love him. He is so cold. Ever since he came to our village, we have not had any corn or flowers to grow." The young man told her to take the bundle of corn with her and do not throw away the husks outside your door, and I will bring you more. Then, he left for his home in the South.

Co-Chin started home. Along the way, she met her sisters. They helped her carry the bundle of corn. When they got home, her father asked about who gave them the corn. Co-Chin didn't know. She described the young man to her father. Her father said, "It is Miochin." Bring him home with you tomorrow. Miochin is the Spirit of Summer.

Co-Chin met Miochin the next day. They went to Co-Chin's village. That evening, Shakok returned home to find Miochin there. He told Miochin to come out and meet. Shakok was very angry to find him there. He told Miochin that he would destroy him. They would have to fight.

Both of them agreed to fight in four days. The victor would win Co-Chin. On the first day, Miochin sent an eagle to his friend, Yat-Moot, asking him to come to help him in the fight with Shakok. On the second day, Miochin sent for all his summer animals of the South; birds, insects and four legged creatures to help him in the fight. Miochin used the bat as his eyes to see what Shakok was doing. The bat's tough skin would protect it from the cold of Shakok. It could stand the sleet and snow that Shakok would throw at it. On the third day, Yat-Moot started his fires heating small flat stones for the battle to come. Also, Yat-Moot called for storm clouds to come.

Shakok did much the same. Shakok lived in the North. Shakok called for all his winter animals; birds and four legged creatures to come help him. Shakok used the Magpie as his advance observer to see what Miochin was doing.

On the fourth day, Shakok and Miochin met in battle. The battle lasted several days. After nobody could win over the other, Shakok decided to call a truce. It seems that the heat melted the snow, and the cold stopped the thunderstorms. It was no use to continue. Both men agreed to the truce.

To settle the argument, they reached an agreement. One half of the year would be warm, or summer and the other half would be cold or winter. Both agreed to make no more trouble. That is why we have half a year warm and half a year cold. Because Shakok could not defeat Miochin, it was decided that Co-Chin would be Miochin's forever. This made Co-Chin's father happy as well. He would be warm and have more food to eat. The cold had made the land barren.

Nick asked about spring and fall. June laughed saying, "That's another story." We all joined in on that one. I told Nick to take a dip in the spring. It would help his anxiety. Rose said she would go and make sure that Nick had no problems. She would make sure he would get back.

One Feather told June that he would go out into the woods to keep watch tonight. June replied to him that she thought that Midnight and Snow would want to be with each other. "Why shouldn't they be with each other?" June asked. One Feather said the only thing he could. "Yes, we should." June pointed to two bright falling stars that crossed each other in the dark sky. "Those are our stars. We are fated to be together. I don't know why. Destiny does not reveal why. You can only follow where it points. We have no choice. Take my hand and follow me. Our wolves know what destiny is. Now it is our turn to follow it." They could hear their wolves howling. One Feather led June to a special place by a small waterfall. He had put a

51

blanket down over some dried grass. June knew that One Feather felt the same as she did.

Nick fixed his and Rose's tent together. Rose had captured Nick's heart. He had wanted her the moment he saw her. Rose could sense his need for her. Nick was lost and needed someone to help him back. She knew that feeling of lost. She had resisted him too long.

Nick took her hand. She took his in hers. In a short walk, they arrived at the spring. A fever grew inside him. It had been too long. Rose was a very beautiful mature woman. Rose felt Nick's need for her rising. His energy was building encircling her. It was strong. He was pulling her into his passion. She couldn't resist him. It had been too long for her. She needed someone to love her. She didn't care about tomorrow. His energy was exciting her body. She had almost forgotten how it felt. Her energy was starting to match his. Her body was responding to his.

When Nick pulled her close to him, he kissed her fully on her red ruby lips. Sparks flew in his mind. Rose couldn't help herself. She kissed him back with a passion she hadn't felt for many years. He unbuttoned her short purple blouse. Rose had already torn off Nick's shirt. Her heavy breasts were warm to his muscular chest. Their clothes seemed to have a mind of their own. They fell to the ground. Holding each other's hand, they slowly walked into the spring. Instead of the pool being cool, it was warm to their skin. Their combined passion was rising like the mists of the pool into the cool mountain air. They clung to each other as they settled down into the shallow water. The warm water enveloped their bodies. Time stopped; only the stars moved in the sky above. Their bodies tingled from the energy that had been trapped inside of them. Their skin started to glow.

They had fought their feelings for each other too long. Now it was time for them to become as one. There was no need for thought, just need for feeling and touching. They tried hard to slow the passion down. Their bodies knew different. Rose said a sacred love spell as they melted into each other to become one. Nick surrendered to her every wish and want.

Moses asked Lo Ming if he could put their tents together. Lo Ming replied to him that that would be fine with her. Moses had felt that something was not quite right with her. She seemed distant. He could not read her mind. He started to wonder if she was hiding something from him. They had been very close in the Spring journey. He decided to take it slow. Perhaps, the threat to her life had left her with some psychological issues. Moses shook his head. He didn't think so. She was a warrior.

I had told everyone to get some sleep. It was only a few hours till daybreak. We would have to be on the trail as soon as possible to make the deadline for the Council meeting.

Mary was standing by her tent. I went over to her to see how she was doing. She was staring into the sky. She didn't notice me. I touched her arm, so I wouldn't startle her. At that moment, I saw a young boy's face. I had seen that face before. It was the boy that the Red Woman was raising. The Red Woman said that his mother had been hurt very seriously. She was going to raise him by herself. She would be like his grandmother. I jumped back from Mary after seeing that vision in my mind. "John, you saw the boy's face, too," Mary whispered to me. I nodded, "Yes." "How is that we both saw him?" she asked. I could only reply, "I don't know. Maybe, I saw him once before somewhere. Who knows in this place? The Land of the Eagle Feathers has a way of its own."

Mary seemed so fragile as she looked into my eyes. She was still lost and trying to find some sense out of the happenings these last few days. I felt a desire to put my arms around her. For some reason, I wanted to protect her and calm her fears about the future. Mary turned to go into her tent. Her

53

demeanor had changed in an instant. "Don't worry about me. I am my father's daughter. I will find out about my past by myself. I don't need your help, John," she sarcastically replied back. She may have said that to make me think she was tough. She didn't realize that I saw a small tear in her right eye before she turned to go inside her tent.

I had heard about this forest in legends. They say that these woods brings out the hidden passion of those who visit here. I don't know why that I had the urge to hold Mary in my arms. I never try to reason about all things here in this land. I found that everything has a purpose. I just go with the flow of the moment.

It was close to morning when Nick and Rose woke up in their tent. Rose was sleeping with him under their blankets. He enjoyed the feeling of her warm soft body next to his skin. His right arm was around her nude body. They were in a spooning position. He pulled her close to him. He had mixed feelings about what had happened last night. He couldn't help it. He remembered his night with Shanna weeks ago. She was once the love of his life. He knew that he loved both women. He needed Rose to help him with his issues. Was that why he was drawn toward Rose? He could feel that Rose needed him as well. Were they two people that needed each other for different reasons? Last night in her sleep, Rose must have been dreaming. He heard her say the name Zan. Was Zan her long lost love?

Rose woke when Nick had pulled her closer to him. She enjoyed his warm body next to hers. She remembered how passionate he had been with her last night. She felt a little guilty about their lovemaking. It was almost like she needed to feel like a woman in love again. It didn't matter to her. You take life as it gives life to you. In her heart, she knew that Zan had been the love of her life. Would she ever see him again? She also knew that Nick needed her much like she needed to

care for him. She would see how this would go. She was
worried about one thing. She should have never been able to
see Nick and Shanna in her crystal ball together. It is said that
you can never use your powers for your own gain. For now,
that didn't matter to her. Who knows their fate? She had
learned not to question everything in life. Destiny has its own
way of guiding your path.

Rose turned her body toward Nick's. Nick started to say
something. Rose put her finger on Nick's lips to stop him from
saying anything. She whispered to him very softly, "We both
need each other. We will always have a special bond. Let's
just see what destiny has in store for us. Don't worry about
tomorrow. It will come too soon." Nick nodded his head and
kissed Rose on her ruby lips. She is right. Rose is always right.

Nick had fixed a quick breakfast of oatmeal with pieces of
dried fruit. Everyone noticed that he had a smile on his face.
That was something we had rarely seen. Rose seemed as
cheerful as ever. It didn't take much to figure out why. June
and One Feather had joined us. Moses and Lo Ming were
together. Whatever had been troubling them seemed to be
behind them or they must of have declared a truce. Antonio
was not in a good mood. I knew what was bothering him.
Angela was not here. Mary was more talkative. I could tell
that her confidence was back. She seemed to be a little short
with me. I still had a lingering feeling about last night. Maybe
this was her way of hiding it.

It wasn't long before we were on the trail again. One Feather
told us that it would be about sundown when we would reach
the sacred Eagle Mountain's base. We would have to pick up
the pace today.

One Feather had set a fast pace. We only rested a couple of
times. We traveled through long flowery meadows rich with
green grass. Herds of deer, elk and buffalo were grazing on the
grass. To save time, Nick passed out his homemade energy

bars to everyone. We didn't even stop for lunch. We could see that we were getting closer to the sacred mountain. This seemed to encourage us to hike faster. It was starting to get dark when we arrived at the base of the mountain. We had camped here on our spring journey.

June noted one thing about the valley we had just crossed to get here. She asked, "Why had the flowers in this valley between the mountains turned bright red? When we left here last season, they were white and yellow." One Feather replied, "The only one who can tell you why is John. He knows why. I cannot tell you because this is for him to tell. Tomorrow, you will go up to the Council Meeting. I must go now to meet with the Grand Elder and the Red Woman on the mountaintop." As One Feather turned to go, June grabbed him and gave him a big fat kiss. Everyone couldn't help but smile. One Feather's face turned red with embarrassment.

We set up camp as we always did. Moses, Lo Ming and Mary went to the mountain stream nearby and caught several trout. Rose and Nick picked some spices from several plants in the meadow. Antonio had discovered some wild potatoes growing in a small field. He dug them up. Nick told everyone that he would have a feast fit for a king for us tonight.

Nick was right. With the assistance of Rose, he cooked up a grand meal for everyone. I reached into my pack. I pulled out a bottle of white wine. "This is a special bottle of wine. A wizard from the Louisiana swamps gave me this bottle. He said only to open it on special occasions. It is kind of magical. It never runs dry. I only have to cork it, and it fills up again. It will give out different types of wine based on the food you eat with it. My guess is that it will be White Sangria tonight, to match the fish." It was White Sangria as I poured wine into each one's cup. Rose looked into my eyes as I poured her cup. She whispered to me that she knew who had given it to me. She said, "My father had one."

The night sky was clear and full of stars. It was a perfect night to be outside. June waited for a long time to ask her question to me. It was about midnight. I told everyone that we had better get some sleep. Tomorrow would be a long day. As I rose from my seat next to the log I had used as a backstop, June finally asked the question I dreaded to answer. "Why are the flowers so red in the valley?" she asked.

I opened my wine bottle and took a deep drink. Everyone straightened up to listen to my answer. I told them that I would only give a short answer to that question. "Many years ago, the Dark Ones had somehow gained entrance to The Land of the Eagle Feathers. I had been sent by the Council to stop them and force them to leave. I had many brave people with me. It was a hot summer day when they arrived to meet my forces. I can still remember how the Dark Ones' army looked as they marched into the valley. Their flags were bright red flowing in the Summer breeze. Their armor was shiny black. I had surrounded the valley with my forces. We attacked them at midday. The battle lasted several hours. We won the battle, and their forces broke and ran. It was a costly victory. Many things happened that day, good and bad. Many of my friends died. I died too. The Council gave me life for my deeds. I am only half of what I used to be. The Council declared that no more blood would ever be shed in battle in this valley ever again. Each Summer, the flowers in this valley turn bright red to salute the sacrifice of those whose blood was shed here. Never ask me anymore about this. The memories are too painful. That is all I will ever say about this." I turned and went to my tent. Tears were flowing down my face.

Morning came early. Nick had breakfast fixed. After eating, we were headed up the mountain to attend the Council Meeting. The climb up the mountain was slow. It had rained, and the slope was slippery and muddy. Moses lead the way. It was dark by the time we reached the mountaintop. We pitched camp. It would be soon when we would attend the Council Meeting. After a quick meal, we headed to the meeting place.

When we reached the meeting place, torches had already been lit around the top of the mountain. We seated ourselves to wait for the meeting to start. A flute could be heard in the distance. Drums started beating to an ancient rhythm. Eight strong braves appeared. They were carrying four baskets. It took two braves to carry one basket. In the background, the flute and drums became louder. A large thunderclap shook the mountain. A flash of lightning blinded us. As we started to focus our eyes again, each brave had two rattlesnakes in their months. The baskets were open. They had been filled with rattlesnakes. Each basket had snakes moving down their sides.

The members of our group were taken back by the scene in front of them. They were not expecting something like this. Antonio did not like snakes. He started to get up. Moses placed his hand on his shoulder. Moses could tell that other people were apprehensive about what was happening. June had heard of her Elders telling stories about this dance. It had been outlawed in her tribe. It took great courage to take part in this dance. Moses spoke to the group, "Do not be afraid. The dance is for us. It is a very sacred dance. It is done for only a few. The rattlesnake that I talked to before said they were inspired by our great deeds. They want to help us, not hurt us. Please calm yourselves and remain seated."

A Great Medicine Man appeared. He was chanting in rhythm to the music. An eagle feather was in his hand. As he moved and swayed, the rattlesnakes moved with the movements of the feather. The Snake Dance had begun.

The eight braves divided into four groups. Each had a basket of snakes in front of them. Each had a rattlesnake in their mouth. This was an ancient dance from the Western United States. After much dancing and swaying, the music and chanting stopped.

The Great Medicine man looked at us. "The honor of this dance is to honor you who come to help The Land of the Eagle Feathers. It is to show our faith in you. There is one of you who we honor. He is the one who talks to animals. Our Great Snake told us of his power and kindness. We honor him." The Great Medicine Man pointed at Moses. All the snakes moved toward him. Moses and Lo Ming did not move. Antonio and the others were not so sure. The snakes were almost on top of us when they stopped in front of Moses. They moved to form a circle. Two braves stopped at four points outside their circle.

In the center of the circle was a large rattlesnake. It moved toward Moses. The snake stopped at Moses' feet. Moses looked into the snake's eyes. They seemed to be talking to each other. The Great Medicine Man moved his feather back toward the center of the clearing. The snakes and braves moved in unison to the center. The braves took the rattlesnakes from their mouths. They placed each of their snakes in one of the four directions of the compass and pointed for the snakes to follow them in that direction. They told the snakes to carry their prayers with them so that all may prosper and have a long life. A group of snakes went with each of the braves that faced one of the four directions: West, East, North and South, carrying their prayers with them. The Great Medicine Man spoke, "May our prayers be carried far in the great circle of Mother Earth." A loud thunderclap shook the valley. A flash of lightning followed, blinding us. When our eyes cleared, all was gone. In their place was the Red Woman.

Even though they had seen her before, this was different. The Red Woman was like a goddess of nature. She carried herself with pride and had an air of nobility about her. Her appearance told them that she was so much more than they had realized. Her voice sang to them like a mountain songbird greeting the morning light. "Behold to you all, I was sent to answer some of your questions. Knowledge is important to understand this land called The Land of the Eagle Feathers," she stated as her eyes pierced the darkness. They could see the moon and bright stars reflecting in her dark eyes. It was as if time and earth stood still. The full moon beamed its rays of light and focused just on her.

"Now is the time to gain more knowledge about this Land of the Eagle Feathers. You have proven by your deeds that you are worthy to know more. In this land, the Eagle feather is most sacred. Only our spiritual leaders such as our Great Medicine Men or Elders possess them. I, the Red Woman, can be the only one that can speak and give them out to others. They are a reward to those that are brave, selfless and respectful. They are given to those that have performed great deeds of bravery in protecting this land. You must understand the nature of the eagle feathers to understand their importance and power.

The colors of the Eagle feathers are black and white with traces of gold. These colors symbolize the nature of all things. They symbolize those opposites that exists in everything in the universe around us like daylight and darkness, summer and winter, and birth and death; the range of all of the wonders of the universe that lies between the spectrum of these colors.

It is on the Sacred Eagle Feathers that prayers are carried to the Great Spirit as the Eagle soars high into the skies above, beyond the moon, the planets and the stars. She pointed to the full moon. There was a silhouette of an eagle flying across its yellow shape against the moonscape.

An eagle feather has great healing powers. It can cure both physical and mental sickness. There are rules to those that possess it. An eagle feather must be displayed with reverence and respect. Never should an eagle feather touch the ground. If it does, only a holy medicine man can pick it up and restore it back to you.

She had stopped talking. Slowly and very carefully, she stared at each member of the group. As her eyes met each of them, they felt as if she was searching their souls and spirits trying to find something unknown. Suddenly, each one felt something in their hands. It was a sacred Eagle Feather.

"Antonio, have you the translation of *The Book of Spring*? You must give it to me. Antonio lifted up his shirt and took out the book with its translation and gave it to her. As he handed it to her, their fingers touched. Instantly, Antonio saw many visions in his mind. Some were good, and some were terrible. Antonio knew that the Red Woman had touched him on purpose because she wanted to read his mind. It was like someone turning the pages in a book and stopping at certain chapters to study them more. As her final words rang out, an eagle appeared and touched the feather in her hand, and they disappeared into the night.

The Great Elder appeared. With him were One Feather and a boy about the age of twelve. He said, "You have done a great deed by finding *The Book of Spring.* Now you must take the knowledge you have gained in the book and find *The Book of Summer.* You will have to put the pieces of the riddle together. Time is short. You must find the book using the clues from *The Book of Spring.* You have only four days to obtain the book and leave this land or *The Book of Summer* will be turned to ashes. If you do not accomplish this, all will be lost. Go in haste and find the book. We have put our trust in you. There will be many dangers you will face if you obtain the book. I hope destiny brings you back here the first day of Fall for the next book. May the Great Spirits of our land be with you." A great beam of light focused on him. They all faded into the light and disappeared. Antonio was the first to speak. "We better get started." That was all that needed to be said.

Chapter IV
Let's find the book:
Where is it hidden?

The sun was fighting the clouds in the distant Eastern Green Mountain Range. Slowly, the sky turned a golden color. The valleys around Eagle Mountain were filled with clouds. It made a scene of mountains with the low clouds in the valleys like a group of islands surrounded by lakes and seas. Lo Ming commented that it remained her of the islands off Vietnam. Mary thought it reminded her of the lakes of Minnesota in the Spring. Nick had the breakfast done. It was dried eggs and some cornbread with blackberry preserves.

We were seated in the circle around the campfire. June was the first to speak, "What is our plan for finding *The Book of Summer*?" Antonio replied, "Each of you had been given a passage from *The Book of Spring.* You were instructed to read the passage and to pick out something that could lead us to *The Book of Summer.* The one thing that you didn't know was the order that I gave the passages out. The order that I gave them out determines points or locations in The Land of the Eagle Feathers."

"That was very clever. If anyone ever got a hold of all the passages you sent, they wouldn't know how the map to the book could be drawn," stated Moses. "How are we to find the locations that we each picked out in our passage?" asked Mary. Antonio replied, "Ask John for that answer, not me."

I told the group that I had an answer for that question. "Over there is our let's say tour guide. He knows every mountain, tree, river, valley, lake and maybe blade of grass in this land. What he does not know, I know." I pointed to One Feather. Out of the corner of my eye, I could see June smile. "This is how it will work. Antonio will ask each of you by order of how he gave out the passages what location or a description of a location or what words you chose as important. After we get to that location, he will ask the next one. Then we would go to the next and so on until we find the last location. This way, nobody will have all the clues and make a map of their own. The starting point is where you are seated."

Antonio looked at Lo Ming, "What do you say, Lo Ming?"

Lo Ming stated my passage was:

The Spirit Lives On and On and On

Some say, it's always been
When you feel the touch of the wind
You feel the touch of one who's gone
The Spirit lives on and on and on

Riding the stars in the sky
Flying so low, flying so high
Hiding in the leaves of the tree
Flying so close, flying so free

Singing these songs of an ancient race
Touching your body, touching your face
Playing in the spray of a fountain
Flying to the valley, flying to the mountain

Telling the stories of those left behind
Visiting your world, visiting your mind
Dreams coming in the still of the night
Flying to the left, flying to the right

Visiting the land of those who know
Touching your mind, touching your soul
Only known to the minds that understand
Flying to the mountain, flying to the land

She stated, "It was easy. The words that jump out of the page to me were: **Hiding in the leaves of the tree, Playing in the spray of a fountain, Flying in the valley, Flying to the mountains and Flying to the left and flying to the right.**" One Feather asked her what that meant. Lo Ming told him, "Where there is a great waterfall with a valley between two mountains with one mountain on the left and one mountain on the right. One other thing that there must be a cemetery there with a tree that the wind blows its leaves because a line indicated it by the words: **Telling the stories of those left behind.**"

One Feather thought for a moment without talking. "There is only one place like that in this land. It is a sacred valley called **The Land of the Dead**." June interrupted by saying, "I have heard of such a valley in my studies with Great Shamans. There is a legend about that valley. It is said to be guarded by a powerful small band of Shamans called **Keepers of Life.** They will never let anyone into the cemetery. They are to guard it, so nobody can desecrate the cemetery and disturb the dead. There is a large tree there that grows in the middle of the cemetery. It has large green leaves that stay green all year. It is said that the leaves never stop waving in the wind. The leaves represent the life of each of us. The leaves must always keep waving. If a leaf stops waving, it will turn brown and fall from the tree. That means someone has died."

I told everyone to get packed. It will take us half a day to get there. I know where this valley is. Unfortunately, I have been there. We will need all our powers to get to a piece of a golden key that one of the leaves holds. That was another thing that Antonio failed to tell you. Each point or location will give us a piece of a Golden Key. We must have all the pieces of the key to open a cave where *The Book of Summer* is hidden. Take only your weapons and food. We will need to travel fast. We don't have much time. We leave in 10 minutes.

Everyone was ready to go in 10 minutes. One Feather was not around. I told everyone that we needed him to help guide us. I was not so sure that I could find The Land of the Dead without him. I told our group that I was worried that we would not have enough time to find *The Book of Summer* and get it out of The Land of the Eagle Feather in time. It was going to take at least one day to get to The Land of the Dead.

In about 15 minutes, One Feather finally arrived. On his back were several coils of rope. I knew what he had in mind. We would save several hours by taking a very dangerous way down the mountain. The east face of Eagle Mountain was a cliff. It was almost straight down with little to hang on to. With the ropes, we could repel down the cliff saving valuable time.

There was only one problem. Rose quickly stated that she was afraid of heights. Nick looked at Rose and tried to reassure her that he would take care of her on the way down. I was surprised that nobody else had any problem going down the side of the cliff. Rose said she would do it if Nick would assist her.

We hiked over to the far eastern side of the mountaintop. It was a good four thousand feet down to the valley below. I had to admit that if you were afraid of heights, it would be a big challenge to tackle a cliff like this one. I asked Rose if she thought she could do this. She replied, "When I was a kid, I fell down the side of a small cliff. I never did get over that fall. I would dream about it every night for weeks. I will not let our group down. The only thing I ask is that I go last with Nick.

Antonio examined the mountainside. Taking a stick, he drew a map of the cliff. "I once was a guide in the Swiss Alps many years ago," Antonio stated. "I suggest that we go this route down." One Feather nodded in agreement. Antonio tied several of the ropes together. With four ropes tied together, he had about 300 feet of rope line. He pointed to a small outcropping about 250 feet down. "There is enough room on that ledge for all of us. If you are careful, we can scale down the side of the cliff to that outcropping, and we would only have two more repels before we could reach that narrow trail to the bottom. I will go first," Antonio confidently said.

Antonio made himself a harness. He was about to explain to the others how to use it to repel, but everyone except Rose told him that they knew how to repel. Nick said that he would take care of Rose. Antonio threw the ropes over the cliff. Attaching himself to the main rope, he started to repel down. It seemed to take Antonio only a few seconds to get down to the outcropping. Antonio tugged the rope to signal it was time for the next one to come down. To save time, Nick had fashioned several harnesses for the rest of us. Rose noted that Nick was one short. Nick replied, "Now Rose, we will be going together. The rope is strong enough to hold both of us. You will be tied to my back much like parachutists do." Rose replied back to Nick, "Well, if that doesn't work, I will have good company accompanying me to The Land of the Dead. We will be getting there first." I did appreciate Rose's sense of humor.

All of us had made it to Antonio's ledge except Nick and Rose. We watched as Nick fastened Rose to his back. When he took them over the cliff, we could hear Rose screaming. She seemed to be saying something like, "Stop laughing, you son of a -----." It wasn't long before they were standing beside us. Rose was laughing. "That was almost fun. I should have tried mountain climbing sooner. I guess having a cute, young lad to hold on to made it much more enjoyable," Rose said with a smile. I started wondering if Rose really was afraid of heights.

We made it down the mountain in less than two hours. We hid our ropes to pick them up later. We had a good two more hours to go. One Feather took the lead with June behind him. I told One Feather when we got close to our destination to stop.

We would have to be careful or the Keepers would not be too friendly about us coming.

We moved as fast as possible. We ran part of the way. I was pleased that everyone had done so well. One Feather halted our group about two hundred yards short of our destination. You could see the waterfalls in the distance. It was about 350 feet high. The mist from the falls and the sunlight created a beautiful rainbow. We could see a large tree covered with green leaves in the middle of a cemetery. The cemetery had a great rock wall at least 15 feet high around it. The top of the wall was covered with sharp crystals. There was a large iron gate in the center of the front wall. This was where we must enter the cemetery.

There was only one thing I didn't like about this scene. There were 12 Shaman dressed in white robes trimmed in black with hoods standing by the iron gate. It looked like they knew we were coming.

Moses asked, "What is your plan to get into the cemetery?" I replied, "It is simple we will just knock on the door." They didn't seem to like my plan, but they followed me up to the iron gate anyway.

I got in front of our group and started up to the iron gate. When I was about 15 feet from the Keepers, an older female Shaman walked up to me. "We were expecting you. We have heard of your group, John. They are called **The Keepers of the Yawi.** I see that they are armed with weapons. They are not allowed into the cemetery. As their leader, John, you will be allowed. We know what you want. Only you will be able to obtain it. You were once here a long time ago. We were surprised that you made it back here alive. You will accompany me while your Keepers are fed by our Keepers. It is only the right thing to do. Now follow me, John." I nodded my head. I signaled to Moses to wait for me to return.

The Elder Shaman introduced herself as Heila. She led me by the stones of those buried here. "Each stone tells a story of a great warrior. The tree in the middle of this cemetery holds each person's lifeline. I will show you the one that is yours." We reached the large tree covered with leaves. Heila pointed to a large half-brown leaf on a lower branch of the tree. "John, that is your leaf. Notice that it is turning brown. When the leaf turns completely brown, it will fall off the branch. When it does, it will fall to the ground. You will then die. Since you are considered to be a great warrior, you will be buried here."

"I know what you are saying. The reason the leaf is half brown is that the Council of Elders made it that way when they brought me here after I died in the great battle. They said it was the only way I could come back. I am half ghost and half alive. My only hope is to find *The Book of Winter* and its power. How long do I have?" I asked.

"You have only until the new year. I do have one thing that bothers me. I know it was your destiny to come here. I wonder if you obtain the book, will you be able to handle its power? I know that you feel that the Council was unfair to you. I fear that you may seek some sort of revenge. You are a good man. I hope your heart is still good. I am but a Keeper. Your destiny is written in the stars. I will give you your piece of the golden key."

Heila pointed at a green leaf next to my leaf. It fell into her hands. It contained a gold piece of the golden key. "There is one more thing. If you find *The Book of Summer,* you have only a short time to get it out of this land. When you cross over, you must leave one of your members in The Land of the Eagle Feathers. There will be a terrible earthquake that will destroy some of The Land of the Eagle Feathers. It might destroy the one that you left behind. You must decide which one to leave. You cannot tell the others. It is the price we must pay for the book. I wish you well, John. May the Great Spirits be with you. Now leave this place. You have little time left."

As I left the iron gate to join the others, Rose ran up to me saying, "We cannot leave this place yet. There is another piece of the golden key here." I turned to Heila and asked her, "Is it true what Rose says?" Heila looked at Rose. She studied her for a moment. "You must be Rose. You are known in the mystic world. You have great powers. I was wondering if you would figure out this part of the puzzle. Rose is correct. She is very perceptive. Even I don't know where the next golden piece is at in the cemetery."

Rose chose her words carefully. "My passage was:

The Spirits are Always Watching You

See the star shining bright
It's an Indian brave riding in the night
See the tree swaying in the wind
It's a message the spirits send

It may be hard to understand
Spirits live in an unknown land
No matter what you do
The spirits are always watching you

They come at day or night
They come if you're wrong or right
They have no form or shape
From them, there is no escape

There's nowhere you can run
The spirits know what you've done
There's nowhere for you to hide
The spirits are by your side

When you've done wrong, they'll know
You'll see an unknown glow
So be careful what you do
The spirits are always watching you

You see it was in the first stanza that has the clues.

See the star shining bright
It's an Indian brave riding in the night
See the tree swaying in the wind
It's a message the spirits send

Each famous warrior has their own stone. An Indian brave riding in the night is an Indian who is a spirit. The tree swaying in the wind is the large tree in the cemetery. The brave is one of the greatest warrior chiefs that rode a horse in battle. You, John, know who I am talking about. I read about him when I was a young girl." I asked Heila, "Can we could go back into the cemetery?" Heila motioned for me to come. She told Rose to wait here until we returned.

When we reached the tree, I started to look around at the stones. I saw a stone with a star on top. It was an old friend. I had met him in the Great Plains Indian wars. They said he rode a horse like a crazy man in battle.

I went over to the stone. "You were a great warrior and man. You were my friend. I revenged your death at the hands of those soldiers. Now, I ask you one more favor. I must take the golden piece of the golden key that is in the star on top of your stone. The other great warriors here must rest in peace forever. I will not stop until all are safe." The great stone started to shake. The star shattered on the top of the stone. A gold piece of the golden key landed in the palm of my outstretched hand. "May one day, I see you again and ride with you in the sky.

That day will come soon enough. I have many deeds to do before that time will come, old friend," as I tipped my hat.

Heila took me back to the iron gate. As I turned to leave, she spoke, "If Rose is any indication of the members of **The Keepers of the Yawi**, you have a chance to save this sacred land. We will meet again, John." I tipped my hat to her, "I hope it will be many circles of the moon and sun. You know where I want to rest."

Our group was sitting under a small maple tree out of the hot summer sun. I asked Antonio who was the next person that we need to get clues from. Antonio stated, "June was the next one with clues."

June told us that her passage was:

The Wisdom in *The Book of Spring*

Mother Earth and Father Sky
We come to ask you why
Spring is the season for rebirth
We are all children of Mother Earth

Watch the river flowing South
Look for orange backed trout
Hunt for the split oaken bough
Listen for the gray wolf's howl

The pink moon rising in the sky
Points to where it may lie
The wisdom of the ages is there
Hidden in the den of the bear

The wind will whisper your name
Nothing will ever be the same
Everything old will seem new
Everything false will seem true

It is now and has always been
Listen to the songs of the wind
The voices of the birds will bring
The wisdom of *The Book of Spring*

June stated that we needed to go to a river flowing south that has orange backed trout. There will be an oak tree with a split branch. We will have to wait for the pink moon to rise. When a grey wolf howls at the pink moon, we will watch where it shines. It will shine on a tree den of a bear. The wind will whisper my name. There will be songbirds singing. There is one thing that we need to keep in mind. Things will seem different after we get the next piece of the key.

One Feather stated in sign language that he knew where to lead them. One Feather said that it will be dusk by the time we get there. I nodded to One Feather to lead us to the river. We would have to hurry to make it there before the moon rises.

It took about an hour to reach a river running south. We could see that there were orange trout in the river. Moving as fast as we could, we reached an oak tree with a large, long branch that was split almost in two. The moon was just starting to rise. We stopped and waited. After what seemed hours, a grey wolf in the distance started howling at the pink moon. Beams of moonlight landed high in a large hollow tree about 100 feet away. This had to be the tree. Bears often make their dens in hollow trees. June told us that she would be the one to climb up and get the piece of the golden key.

Moses lifted June up to the nearest branch of the hollow tree. June climbed about 20 feet up the tree trunk. Finally, she reached the bear den in the tree. A gentle wind started blowing through the forest. The leaves of the trees seemed to be making a whispering sound. It was a name. It sounded like the name: June. June reached into the bear den. She felt around for a few moments. She pulled out her arms and in her hands was a small gold chain with a small golden piece attached. She put the chain around her neck. When she did that, songbirds began to sing all through the forest. Their beautiful songs filled the forest. We did nothing but listen to the music. We had the next piece of the golden key. June was soon on the ground. She stated that she would not take off the chain until we reached the cave with *The Book of Summer*.

It was getting too dark to travel anymore. We needed rest before we could go on. Antonio looked at Nick. Nick said, "I guess I am the next one in line. We will have to go to the edge of the forest. My passage was:

It Comes at Night

The sun is starting to set
I'm feeling things I can't forget
They get stronger with the twilight
I know it comes at night

The darkness is starting to appear
The visions are starting to become clear
It's a feeling I can't fight
I know it comes at night

The silence of the dark surrounds me
There's something here I can't see
I can't resist or try as I might
I know it comes at night

I see its vision, and we are together
It touches me with an eagle feather
It makes everything seem so right
I know it comes at night

I see the first break of day
I know it'll have to go away
It'll ride the eagle away in flight
I know it comes at night

The great spirits must have known that it would be night when we got June's piece. I will have to sleep and watch the visions in my dreams. We will need to get up at first light and watch for an eagle in flight. We will have to go in that direction. I am getting very tired."

One Feather led us to the edge of the forest. We made a camp. Nick sat down near a large boulder. He fell asleep quickly. Moses said he would awaken us at first light. Soon, everyone was asleep on the soft grass. It had been a long day.

Rose chose to be near Nick. She knew Nick was dreaming. She watched him turn one way and then the next. He was talking to someone or something. She couldn't stay awake any longer.

It was starting to get light when Moses woke everyone up. June was the first one to see the eagle in flight. It was heading back north toward Eagle Mountain. We watched as it flew out of sight. Nick started to wake up. His eyes were the color of bright blue. They sparkled in the morning light.

"We must go toward the mountains in the direction that the eagle flew. My dream had a great White Owl in it. It got bigger as the night got darker. It said to go to where the White Owl lives. There will be an eagle feather that will float down from the sky. When it touches my hand, that will be where the piece of the golden key will lie," Nick recalled from his dream.

I told the group that must be White Owl Mountain. It is said that a great White Owl lives there. One Feather nodded that he knew where to go. We gathered our stuff and headed toward the mountain to the north. We ate the last of the breakfast bars as we went.

It was about midday when we arrived at the base of the mountain. One Feather took us to the base of a high cliff. There on the top of the cliff stood a great White Owl. Slowly a golden eagle feather appeared high in the sky. Nick watched as it floated down from the sky. He moved with the feather's flight. He ran underneath it as it touched his hand and caught it. He was standing on top of a small flat rock that had gold in it. He lifted the flat golden rock and picked up another piece of the key. The great White Owl hooted as if to signal that Nick had done his job.

Antonio didn't wait. He pointed toward Mary. Mary repeated her passage.

Hidden in Your Mind

Look to the eyes of Father Sky
Wait for the sound of the eagle's cry
Listen to the voice of the wind
That tell you secrets the elders send

Watch for signs from Mother Earth
Listen for the sounds of birth
Wait for the sounds from a bird's nest
That tell you secrets while you rest

North is South, and South is North
Watch for the deer to go forth
Wait for brother wolf to howl
That tell you when the animals bow

Look for the old oak tree
Wait for what you will see
Listen to the leaves that roar
That tell you how to open the door

Look at everything you saw
Watch and listen to it all
Wait for images of a circle
That tell you of nature's miracle

Then only can you know
You're within a stone's throw
Then only will you find
The secrets that are hidden in your mind

Mary stated that we are near the next and last piece of the key. We are within a stone's throw. She looked at One Feather. "Where is North is South, and South is North?" she asked. One Feather picked up a stone and threw it toward the center of the meadow we had just come from. We walked over to where the stone landed. On the ground were rocks lined up like a large compass. The compass was not laid out right. The North was in the position of the direction South, and South is where North was.

Mary had everyone form a circle. As the last of us formed the circle around the compass, visions and images formed in the middle of the circle. An image formed by eagles flying in the sky that looked like two eyes appeared. Then an eagle cry could be heard in the distance. It was replaced by deer running forth out of the circle. The deer vanished into an old oak tree. A wolf's howl could be heard. Mary stated, "The last piece of the key is where nature's miracles happen. It is in the bird's nest in the oak tree. Is not birth the miracle of nature?" Mary went to the oak tree. Reaching up to the bird nest, she reached in and pulled out the last piece of the golden key.

Antonio pointed to the last member of our group. "Moses, it is your job to find where the cave is hidden. Your passage told you that. Moses nodded and said his passage.

The Great Spirit's Land

In the times of the old
There are secrets the spirits hold
A few remain who know the story
Of times of honor and glory

Listen to what the winds say
Listen to the music of the trees' sway
Listen to the echo of the ancient flute
Listen to the message in the Owl's hoot

Look to the direction of the skies
Look to the eagle that flies
Look to the symbols on the rock
Look to yourself to open the lock

Your ears will let you hear the winds
Your ears will hear what the tree sends
Your eyes will see where to go
Your eyes will see what you should know

Oh, Great Father in the sky
Oh, Great Creator up so high
Give him the wisdom to understand
How to enter the Great Spirit's Land

Moses grinned at us. "The first stanza holds the most important clue.

In the times of the old
There are secrets the spirits hold
A few remain who know the story
Of times of honor and glory

This means that to find the book I must become one with **The Land of the Eagle Feathers**. I must go back to the time of creation or in the Outback we call the time of Dreaming. I must meditate with the Old Ones of this land. Much like my forefathers did in Australia in the Outback. They are **the few who know the story**.

The ancient flute is a didgeridoo. This is one of the oldest flutes in the world. If I follow **the secrets of the spirits and hear what they say, my eyes will see.** I will be given **the wisdom to understand the symbols on the rock to open the lock**. This means to unlock the cave's entrance to the book. I will represent all indigenous people and all aboriginal people. That is why nobody else would find the book. They would only think of one group of indigenous people. That's the genius behind the Great Medicine man who hid this book. You will see other things that the passage said as I find my way.

In my pack are the items that I will need to meditate to find the hiding place for *The Book of Summer.* I will go to the time of Dreaming. This will take time. Please do not stop or talk or bother me at any time. Go to the shade of the oak tree over there and look at this side of the mountain. You will see symbols and other signs on the cliff wall. No matter what happens, do not interfere with what I am doing. Now, I must change into my tribal clothing. I will find the sacred book. First, give me the pieces of the key. Now go and be seated on those rocks by the oak tree."

Moses stripped off his clothes and put on a loincloth made of possum and human hair. The hair was probably his mother's hair mixed with his. The hair was hung in rows down each side of the loincloth. Out of his pack, he took out body paint and a didgeridoo (an ancient Aboriginal Flute) which was about a 100 cm or three feet long. It had colorful symbols of animals and birds on it. One symbol was a bird flying.

Moses started painting his body with symbols in white or other colors. Some were stars, moons and an eagle flying. A few of the symbols looked like spirits of animals, men, women and children. The sun was getting very hot. Moses sat down in a bare spot that was full of red sand. He took some of the red sand and made the symbol for a meeting place which is a circular symbol. He also made prints of large bird tracks walking in front of him.

He picked up the didgeridoo and started to play. The didgeridoo made very low sounds. He played an ancient rhythmic prayer to the great spirits of all Aboriginal People. He swayed like a tree as he played. The sound had a calming effect on all who heard it. Soon we all became part of the ceremony. We saw what Moses saw. Visions of the Dreaming covered the cliff. We saw Man coming from under the earth and animals being born. Stars forming in the heavens with birds flying down from above shone brightly in the rocks of the cliff.

A rattlesnake appeared near Moses. Its rattles beat with the same rhythm of his spirit song. Moses' eyes were opened wide. He kept swaying with the rhythm as more symbols flashed on the cliff wall. I recognized some of them. Some symbols were from ancient tribes of the Middle East and Africa, and some symbols were Tibetan, Mongolian, Aztec and Native American. It seemed that all the indigenous people of the world were represented on the cliff.

A vision of spirits covered the cliff wall replacing all the other symbols. They were talking in many ancient languages. They turned and talked to Moses. Moses stopped playing the didgeridoo. He stood up. A hoot of an owl shook the mountain. High above us a golden eagle appeared flying down as if he was the messenger from the Great Creator, landing in front of Moses. The eagle disappeared. The tracks of the great bird that Moses had drawn in front of him started to move toward the cliff. A flute in the distance could be heard playing the same song that Moses had played. Moses took the pieces of the golden key from a pouch on his waist. In his big right hand, they melted together forming a complete key. He followed the eagle tracks to the side of the cliff. His eyes were wide, staring at a small rock that protruded out of the cliff. The eagle tracks stopped at the wall. A great gust of wind blew sand and encircled Moses. Moses took the golden key and with all his might, thrust it into the rock before him. All became silent, and not a sound could be heard except for the wind.

A small cave opened before Moses. Moses walked into the cave. We waited for several minutes, daring not to move. Moses walked out of the cave covered in red dust carrying a book that was covered with precious stones and gems. He had in his outstretched arms *The Book of Summer.* He walked over to Antonio and said, "The great spirits of all indigenous people entrust you with this sacred book. They said that you know what to do." Antonio took the book and put it in a special leather bag that he had been carrying. The bag was covered with symbols.

Moses walked back to where he had been sitting. He seated himself. He picked up the Didgeridoo and finished playing the prayer song. Joining him was a flute in the distance. When Moses finished the song, he looked up into the sky, he said, "I understand." Moses fell back and passed out into a deep sleep. A flying eagle that was above us flew up higher into the sky until it disappeared into the clouds as if it was carrying back the words of Moses to **the Great Creator**.

We let Moses sleep for about an hour. During that time, we discussed how to get the book out of The Land of the Eagle Feathers. We did not have enough time to go back to the Eagle Mountain to get the rest of our packs. One Feather spoke to June's mind. He said that if they could contact the Little People, they might help us. There were many Little People that stayed around the top of the Sacred Eagle Mountain to protect it.

June took out one of her hawk feathers. Pointing to the sky, she said a few words. It wasn't long before a large brown hawk appeared in the sky. June had taken out a sheet of paper and gave it to One Feather. One Feather had drawn a series of pictures that would tell the Little People to take our packs down to the base of Eagle Mountain to where we had camped. The large brown hawk landed on June's forearm. One Feather tied the note to the Little People to the hawk's leg. June instructed the hawk to find the Little People and to give the message to them.

I told our group that many cultures have stories of Little People. I had seen them once in The Land of the Eagle Feathers. Here, they are larger than most cultures. They are about half the size of a full-grown adult man or three feet tall or less. For their size, they can be very fierce and aggressive warriors. They could do the job of getting our packs down the mountain.

One Feather told June that it would take about five hours for us to get back to our campsite at the base of Eagle Mountain. I told Lo Ming to wake up Moses from his sleep. We needed to get going if we were to get there before it is dark.

It took a little persuasion to awaken Moses. Lo Ming had to pour a full canteen of water on Moses to awaken him. Moses jumped up with a start. He started to swing at the first thing he saw. Luckily for Lo Ming, she was too fast to get hit. Moses apologized to her about swinging at her. Lo Ming told him that the next time she would not be so nice. She pointed to a spring that was flowing out of the cliff. "Go get cleaned up, you are one dirty soul, or I will do it myself," she said. Moses didn't say a thing. He almost fell as he tried to walk over to the spring. Lo Ming said, "I guess I will have to help you anyway." She grabbed him under his arm and helped him to

81

the small waterfall of the spring. We could hear her saying to him, "Now, you have got me dirty, and I will have to wash too." We were all glad that they were out of sight of us.

In about an hour, we were on the trail to Eagle Mountain. One Feather and June were in the front, leading the way. We were all smiling because you couldn't help but see the grin on Moses' face at the back of the group. It appeared that more than cleaning was done at the spring.

We arrived at Eagle Mountain just before dark. A group of Little People had put up our tents and had a campfire going. They were cooking us some fish with some wild rice. Chief Lohand and his wife, Lakana, greeted us when we arrived. They told us that they had been honored to assist us in our quest. There were about twenty in the group that had brought the packs to us. They said that they would stay and eat with us. It wasn't long before we made a feast of the fish and rice. The Chief and his wife were great hosts. They told stories about their ancestors. We enjoyed Lakana's stories the best. She had a great sense of humor. Her funny stories about her husband had us all laughing so hard our stomachs hurt. Too soon, they bid us goodbye and left. Everyone knew that we had two long days of journey to get to the tunnel. There were only two days left before *The Book of Summer* would turn to ashes if we didn't get it out of The Land of the Eagle Feathers.

It was getting light when One Feather woke the camp. Nick had already fixed us some flatbread with homemade syrup made from some blackberries and bee honey he had found. He did well to get the honey. He had only two stings on his hands.

We headed down the trail. It would be a long day. We made good time. One Feather was still with us. I let Moses lead. I had One Feather and June in the rear.

It was shortly after noon when were arrived at our other camp from a few days ago. I motioned for Moses to lead on. I told him that we should get as close as possible to the tunnel before we stopped for the night. There was a good campsite about six miles up the trail. It had good water and a warm spring. Nobody seemed to mind that we were pushing on to the tunnel. They knew what was at stake.

Moses saw the place that I described to him. It only took us three hours to reach it. We had camp set up quickly. I noticed that Nick and Rose seemed to be getting along better the last few days. Our group as a whole had fared well. Lo Ming and Moses were both talking to each other, if you could call that talking. In this land, lovers could talk to each other's minds without saying a word. Antonio was his normal self. He was a man of conversation. Of course, June and One Feather were two young people in love. Mary was still a little too quiet. She had a hard edge about her. She was polite to everyone. When I tried to talk to her, she would make our conversations as short as possible.

Nick told everyone that the meal tonight would be a stew of jerky and some dried vegetables he had kept in his pack. After supper, we took our turns washing and relaxing in the warm springs. We were sitting by the campfire when Rose came out of her tent upset. She said that she needed to have a meeting with all of us.

"I went into my tent to check on a sound I heard in my small crystal ball bag. It is set to sound an alarm if one of us is in imminent danger. It was the alarm. I took out my small crystal ball. On its face was the image of Moses, he was face down in a pool of blood. Lo Ming was there crying and yelling saying, "Why did you kill him?" My best guess is that it was somewhere in the Outback. It looked dusty and like a desert. The only thing I know is that if Moses goes back with us, there is a good chance he will die. We must have him stay here. He could live with One Feather until we return. Remember, we must have everyone alive to find the next book," stated Rose.

Moses immediately protested, "Don't worry about me, I will be fine. Nobody will be able to get me in the Outback. Besides, I need to meet with my mother to straighten some things out. Lo Ming didn't agree with Moses. "You should not be so hardheaded, Moses. If Rose says you are not safe, then you should listen to her. If it was me, you would make me stay here. You know nobody can get to you here." Moses looked at Lo Ming and took her by the hand. "Let's go to our tent and talk about it. If I change my mind by the time we get to the tunnel, I will let everyone know. There is only one person here that would be able to convince me in staying behind. Lo Ming is the only one I will listen to." With that said, Moses took her by the hand to their tent.

I looked at everyone and said, "It is Moses' decision to stay or go. I think Lo Ming is right. He should stay here. He would be safer. Let's get some sleep. Tomorrow will be a very trying day for all of us."

Lo Ming pulled Moses close to her. It was too warm for their clothes in the tent. Moses talked to Lo Ming with his thoughts. He told her that he loved her. She repeated that and more. She told him that she did not want him to get hurt or die. Tears started running down her face. Lo Ming knew one thing: Rose was usually right in her predictions of the future. Moses told her not to worry. We do not know what tomorrow will bring. Our destiny is that we are together tonight. He kissed her passionately on her lips. He whispered how beautiful she was. Lo Ming wanted tonight to be special. She took the lead in their lovemaking. She touched him in many sensitive places.

Her knowledge of Tao was very extensive. He felt her hands and tongue caressing his body. Lo Ming took out some exotic lotion and slowly spread over his hot body. She took out another small bottle of different lotion and spread it on hers. She whispered to him to lick some of it off her body. He chose her breasts to kiss and lick off the lotion. She did the same to him but much lower.

He started to feel that he could feel her body as if he were part of her. She could feel his excitement running through his body as it was her own. She laid on top of his naked body. The lotion was mixing together. They could not tell which sensations were their own or the other's. She slowly let herself down. She could feel him inside her. Their bodies had become one. The lotions were melting them together. She could feel his pleasure, and he could feel hers. They moved their bodies in an ancient Tao rhythm: not too fast and not too slow. Their bodies became hotter and more electric with each of their movements. They were matching each other. She knew his passion for her, and he matched hers. It was so intimate and so complete. They soon knew what each other felt when their orgasms reached their peak. Their bodies told each other how it felt for the other. It was too erotic to describe.

One Feather woke me at first light. I was very confused about what Rose had said to us the night before. I had planned to leave Moses here in The Land of the Eagle Feathers. He would have the best chance to survive an earthquake or whatever was in store for this land when the book leaves with us. All I knew was that Heila said that it was what had to be. I had to choose one to stay behind. I guess that was now an easy choice.

It took us the better part of the day to reach the tunnel's entrance. Moses said he had to go back. He needed to see his mother. It was too important to stay here. Lo Ming was not happy about his decision to go back. She was still trying to persuade him to stay.

Antonio had the book safely hidden on him. Not knowing what would happen when he entered the tunnel, I put him in the middle of our group. The tunnel was a few feet up a bank of sandy soil. It would be easy to slip down the bank.

One Feather started helping each one up the sandy bank toward the tunnel's entrance. First to reach the entrance and enter was Mary. She was followed by Nick and Rose. June was next. She gave One Feather a quick kiss on his check and told him she would be back soon. Antonio was next. He would be followed by Lo Ming and Moses. I was supposed to be the last inside.

Nobody knew about what was going to happen. I had not said a word to anyone. As Antonio passed the entrance of the tunnel, a loud noise echoed down the valley below. The earth started to shake. Fire could be seen on top of one of the mountains in the distance. The valley was waving like waves in the ocean. Large boulders rose up out of the ground. Rocks and dust started falling around the entrance filling the tunnel. I grabbed Lo Ming. I pushed her inside the tunnel. One Feather ran toward the valley below. I couldn't see anything. I had to run to get out of the way of the rocks. You could hear only a person shouting, "Who pushed me out of the tunnel?" There was no mistaken it. It was Moses's voice. We all ran further inside the tunnel. I pulled out my flashlight to try to see. Our group was standing together in the tunnel a few feet from me. Antonio looked around. The tunnel behind us was blocked. There were only rocks and dirt piled high closing it completely. Antonio said what we all were thinking, "Where is Moses?"

Chapter V
Things are not right:
Who is left behind?

Lo Ming was beside herself about Moses being gone. She ran over to the blocked passage. She lifted some of the rocks and was trying to dig her way by hand. Antonio ran over to her and pulled her back. Lo Ming was in tears. Antonio told her that they could do nothing. It would take dynamite and other explosives to clear out the end of the tunnel to get back to The Land of the Eagle Feathers. He reassured her that Moses was a warrior and knew how to survive in this type of situation. He had probably been able to get out of the tunnel before the rest of the tunnel caved in.

June asked if I had seen what had happened to One Feather. She had witnessed the earthquake that was starting in The Land of the Eagle Feathers. "John, did you see what happened to One Feather?" she asked. I replied, "Yes, he was running down the valley as fast as he could. I am afraid that I lost sight of him. The earthquake was tearing up the valley, and the mountains were on fire. One thing that I do know, One Feather is smart. He is a survivor. I would bet my life on both him and Moses surviving. They are probably trying to figure a way to survive until we come back."

Nick looked angry. "I was in Special Forces. We had a belief we lived by. We never left anyone behind. Moses was special to me. He treated me with respect. He taught me many things about life. I once could not save a friend of mine. I will get Moses back one way or another. I will not leave him behind."

I looked at Nick. I chose my words carefully, "Yes, I know. We will come back and get anyone that is left behind. Like it or not, we have many enemies that will stop at nothing to stop us or try to get the books. Moses and One Feather will have to wait until we find another way into The Land of the Eagle Feathers. I have heard of another way into the land. There is only one thing wrong with that. It only opens once a year. By the way I figure, that will be in three weeks. The moon will then be blood red, and a group of stars will be aligned in a circle. There is no other way into this land any sooner."

Antonio added, "What John says is true. I have deciphered some passages in *The Book of Spring* that mentions some other way into The Land of the Eagle Feathers. I must warn everyone. The passages stated that nobody has ever been able to survive using it. They say it is cursed. No matter how we feel, we still must decipher *The Book of Summer* to find the other books. There may be clues in how to get to the other passage. I have a feeling that the reason the passage mentioned the other way into the land had to do with what just happened. It is probably another test that we must go through." I nodded my head in agreement with Antonio. I started to add that they wanted to make it harder without Moses. I thought that the others will figure that out anyway.

Rose stated, "We need to hurry. We don't have much time to get everything done and be back in three weeks. Now, I know it will be the longest three weeks that most of us have ever faced. June and Lo Ming, we will be here for you. I know that it will be harder on you than any of the rest of us. Let's get out of here and get home and get prepared to get through to them in three weeks."

Mary surprised us by adding her thoughts. "I know it will be difficult to wait three weeks. We do not have any choice. I will say one thing. John, I feel that you knew that this was going to happen. I could feel that something was bothering you. There was something in the way that you put together our way into the tunnel. You put Moses next to you at the end of the line. You had the perfect position to push him back. It didn't matter because John knew that someone had to stay back. It was the price we had to pay for *The Book of Summer.* In my world, everything has a price. In The Land of the Eagle Feathers, there are prices that everyone pays." Mary pulled out a small binocular, "You didn't know that I could read lips. I was up on a nearby hill and watched you with Heila in the cemetery. Heila told you that you had to select one to stay, and that The Land of the Eagle Feathers would also have to pay the price to get the book out. **The owl hoots** in Moses' passage gave it away. He was going to be deceived by you."

I looked Mary straight into her eyes. "What you say is true. However, there is only one thing missing. I didn't push Moses out. Maybe, the Great Spirit told him to stay or someone else pushed him. It doesn't matter now. The Land of the Eagle Feathers has its own way of doing things. We may never know. I do only what I must to find the books. That is our quest. What is done is done. Whether you trust me or not, we need to be back in three weeks. This means defying the Council of Elders. We will need to break the rules. We will have to face the Council for that. Personally, I don't care. I will not wait for Fall to come back for *The Book of Fall*. I promised his father and mother that I would protect him. That is what I will do. There is one thing that I know. "Rules are meant to be broken. Isn't that right, Antonio?" Antonio nodded. I wasn't so sure that everyone believed in what I had said. I knew that I had said too much. What they didn't know was that I would have pushed Moses out anyway.

Antonio told everyone that we had no choice. We had to get back to decipher *The Book of Summer.* We could not do anything until then. I warned everyone to be very careful when Antonio said the words that would open the tunnel wall to let us out. When we reached the tunnel wall, we had a surprise waiting for us. Someone had left us weapons. There was a note on the weapons that said: **Be careful, the forest is full of The Dark Ones. They are waiting for you on the other side of the wall about a day's ride from here. You will not have a choice but to fight or die. I have given you some weapons to fight your way back to the Eagle Train Station. Good Luck!** I could see in everyone's eyes that they wanted to fight someone. They were upset with how things were turning out. They were angry about losing Moses and One Feather.

There were two Chinese short swords and one red spear. These must be for you, Lo Ming. Your fighting stick will not last in a battle with the **Dark Ones.** They are usually heavy armored like soldiers of old. She swung her new swords and tried out her spear. Her mastery of these weapons was noted by all. She made herself a backpack for carrying her swords for easy access. There were some more Golden Hawk Feathers for June plus a tomahawk and knife. There was a large broad sword and a military knife. Nick said that those must be for him. He said that he knew how to use them. I nodded in agreement.

In one bag, there were more arrows for Mary's bow. Antonio noted that there was another wand for him. Rose had found a bag of exploding crystals. However, she wanted to have the small bag of crystals that I had found. She walked over to me and asked for the Ruby Eyes of the Snake. "Why do you want them?" I asked. She replied, "They are special. They have powers to take things into another dimension of space and time." I looked at her and said, "If you use them, you will have to go with whatever you use them on." "I know," she carefully replied back. "I am the only one who knows how to use them. If I do, I will get back. I assure you that I wouldn't let anything ever happen to our group. I especially want to get back to finish this quest. I have a personal reason to go back to The Land of the Eagle Feathers." I knew that her personal reason was more than Nick. She knew something about Zan, her first love being trapped in The Land of the Eagle Feathers. "In that case, you can have them," I reluctantly said.

Whoever put these weapons here knew how to get into the tunnel. Nobody should have been able to do that. I told everyone that something was wrong. David would have never sent a force to stop us. It had to be someone higher than him. David would only attack us after we got *The Book of Winter.* David wanted the book for himself.

"Things are going to get very rough. The **Dark Ones** will bring their fiercest warriors. Some of the **Dark Ones** will be human like us, and some of the others will be half man and half creature. You have not seen anything like some of them. The only **Dark One** that commands such a force besides David will bring enough to do the job of killing us and taking *The Book of Summer* for herself. We will be lucky to survive this especially without Moses," I told them.

Mary asked, "Do you know who is in charge of this force?" I answered back, "Yes, she is very ruthless. I had encounters with her before. She definitely wants to see me fail." "Why is that John?" she asked. "It is very simple. I killed her husband," I replied. Nobody asked me any more questions.

We moved up to the tunnel wall. We readied ourselves for whatever would be on the other side. Antonio deciphered the saying on the wall. The wall opened. On the other side was only daylight and a beautiful view of the green mountains. Nothing else was near. Nick took his hand and felt the air. He told us that there was nothing to be afraid of. Nobody was here. We started down the trail to get our horses to get back to the train station. Morning Star had our horses and mules saddled at the foot of the mountain pass. She said she had seen nothing. Rose was surprised to see her prized red stallion. She started to ask Morning Star about it. Rose decided not to ask. She didn't want to know. She was glad to ride him again. We got on our horses to head back. Antonio and the others were puzzled about how calm and peaceful everything was.

On a ridgetop above, the old man and his dog watched. He looked at his dog and said, "Well, I hope our presents that I gave them help them. They will have a fighting chance. Rose will be surprised to see her horse. She will need that horse if she uses the Rudy, I left for her. My friend, we will watch from here. We will see if they have what it takes for the journeys to come. It will only get harder from now on. What do you think?" His old hound dog answered by barking in agreement.

I put Nick in the lead. I told Morning Star to leave and take the back trail back. I didn't want her in any trouble we might get into. We headed toward the hot spring to camp. We camped at the hot spring in late afternoon. I had each of us take a watch in case any **Dark Ones** would attack us. The next morning, Nick fixed us a fine breakfast of dried eggs, bacon and pancakes with syrup. After breakfast, Nick said, "I can feel that they are up ahead waiting for us. I was always good at knowing such things in the army. There is a fight brewing. One person wants John dead. The others just want to spill blood. I can feel it in my bones. When we fight them, don't give them any mercy. They are here for one reason. They want *The Book of Summer*. They want Antonio. When the fight starts, I will become what I once was. Don't let that bother you."

I reminded them that Antonio and the book must be protected. I gave Mary and June that assignment. June looked at everyone. "We have a beautiful day. There's an old Indian warrior saying. "It's a good day to die." I disagreed with that because we are not going to do that today." We mounted our horses.

I put Nick in front with Lo Ming behind him. Rose was in the middle with Antonio being guarded by June and Mary. I took my place in following far behind to guard the rear. When the sun was high in the sky, we took our noon break. We let the horses take a rest while we ate.

As we rode, the forest was becoming thicker with the bushes full of blooms. We were only about three miles from the rail station when Nick stopped. Tall trees lined both sides of the trail. There were many boulders scattered between with thick brush. Nick knew we were in trouble. Not one bird or animal was making any noise. It was complete silence. Silence in a forest can only mean one thing. Something was disturbing the nature of things. That's when all hell broke loose.

In what seemed like a few seconds, the whole forest floor and trees were covered with creatures and soldiers from the **Dark Ones**. Nick was knocked off his horse by a soldier swinging down a rope. Lo Ming took her spear and threw it into the soldier's back. Then she too got hit by two creatures that knocked her off her horse. Getting up, she took out from her backpack her Chinese fighting swords cutting down the two large wolf-like creatures in front of her. Nick had his long sword out and was chopping and slicing at several armed swordsmen in front of him. He sliced, killing two and fighting another. That one was a master swordsman. Nick had his hands full. Rose threw two of her crystals which exploded near a group of the **Dark Ones**. June yelled for Antonio to follow her and for Mary to cover them with her arrows. Antonio took his wand and sent a bolt of lightning down the trail ahead and knocked down several more creatures that blocked the trail.

Mary took aim and hit a swordsman that was about to grab Antonio. June swung her tomahawk, hitting a hairy dark ape like man beside the trail. June took out two of her hawk feathers, sending bolts of lightning on both sides of the trail.

Nick had become a killing machine. Nothing in his path survived. That didn't matter. We were totally outnumbered. I yelled for June to get Antonio to the train station. We would try to hold them off and then follow her. Reluctantly, she and Antonio nodded, riding off in a gallop, knocking and cutting down anything in their path. I turned my horse around and looked to see if anymore were coming down the trail behind us. That's when I saw her. She and another large man dressed in dark leather armor were running toward me. He was what you called a Dark Tigerman. He carried a long spear and sword. His long hair was the color of an Indian Tiger. They were known as the best elite assassins in the **Dark Ones' forces**.

Very few spirits, let alone people, had ever tangled with one and lived to tell about it. Feeling I had no choice, I leveled my Hawken Rifle at him and blew him away. The force of the bullet knocked him back several feet also knocking down Raven. I now had my chance to get her. Feeling the rage of all those years that she had killed my friends and loved ones, I rode down the trail after her. Immediately, she turned and disappeared into the brush of the thick forest. Jumping off my horse, I followed her into the thick lush brush. No one would stop me now. It would be her or me. Soon I realized that she had led me into a trap. I had let my feelings of revenge get the better of me.

Lo Ming and Nick stood with their backs to each other. They were being swarmed over by several members of the **Dark Forces**. Their swords clanked against the swords of their enemies. Explosions were heard throughout the forest as Rose threw her crystals. Nick and Lo Ming were surrounded by six elite Dark Soldiers. They had their swords out. Nick knew that without help they could only hold them off so long. They were better fighters than he had encountered in a long time. He caught one soldier, pulled him toward him and stabbed him in the chest. That's when another soldier saw his chance to slice Nick. Nick started to feel the sword blade cut his leather jacket. He thought that he was going to die. Out of the corner of his eye, he saw Mary firing arrows toward their position. The cutting blade just stopped. He turned to see that the soldier with the sword had an arrow sticking through him right above his heart. Two of the other soldiers had arrows through them as they fell to the ground. That left only two soldiers for them. They made short work of them.

Mary jumped off her horse to take better aim at the other **Dark Forces** in the trees. One by one, she shot them down. Lo Ming and Nick had finally killed the creatures and soldiers around them. Lo Ming pulled out her red spear from a warrior.

They ran toward Mary. All their horses had run up the trail leaving them on foot. **The Dark Forces** stopped attacking. It looked like **The Keepers of the Yawi** had won.

Hearing a loud horn blowing in the distance told them the fight was not over. Down the trail behind them were at least twenty to thirty more Dark Fighters coming straight at them. They were riding wild black horses that were breathing fire from their nostrils. Each horse had armor with sharp steel spikes sticking out carrying a soldier in black armor covered with spikes. Nick looked at the others. Lo Ming stated, "It was an honor to go to battle with you," knowing they would be no match for them on foot.

Out of nowhere appeared Rose on her red stallion beside them. She looked at them and said, "Get to the train station. I will take care of these fighters. Nick, I will return to see you in three weeks." With that said, she took a Ruby Snake Eye out of her bag and galloped directly at the enemy in front of her. When she was only ten yards from them, she threw the Ruby Snake Eye at the lead soldier. There was a great explosion. Wind, trees breaking, boulders shattering, and dust flew up into the air. When the dust cleared, the forest behind them for over two hundred yards had disappeared, leaving only a clearing. Rose and **the Dark Forces** were gone. Only silence remained, and it was deafening.

Nick fell to the ground in despair. Rose was gone. Lo Ming picked him up. She told everyone that they were needed at the train station to guard Antonio. They started running down the trail. Lo Ming was right. They must get to Antonio and June. Surely, there would be **Dark Ones** at the Ranger Train Station. It didn't take them long for them to reach the station. June and Antonio were sitting on the platform by the station building. Around them were several dead Dark Soldiers. June's tomahawk and knife were dripping with blood. In Antonio's hands was a silver sword. All June would say was she never

95

knew that Antonio was a master swordsman. He had taken a sword from one of the soldiers after that soldier had destroyed his wand. Before she knew it, he had finished off at least six soldiers by himself. It only took him 45 seconds to do the job.

Antonio noticed that Rose and John were missing. They asked what had happened. Lo Ming only said she didn't know about John. She would tell him later about Rose. "We must go on with what John wanted us to do. We need to be back here in three weeks. John and Rose can take care of themselves. We should change our clothes and leave the horses under the oak tree. Morning Star will get them."

Everyone took turns using the old water tower tank hose to shower off the dirt and blood from the battle with the **Dark Ones.** It felt good to be clean and in good clothes. The bodies of the **Dark Ones'** forces had become dust after several hours. A cold wind from the North blew away the dust leaving nothing behind. Nick was terribly upset about Rose. He blamed himself for what had happened. The desert spirits had told him in visions that something would happen to Rose. Lo Ming saw that Nick's heart was breaking. She sat down in the old rocking chair beside his on the front porch of the station. Taking his hand, she told him, "It had nothing and everything to do with you. Rose is a strong mature woman. You cannot blame yourself for the decisions she makes. It was hers to make. Not yours. You are young. You will learn in the years to come. Fate has a journey of its own. You must follow it and learn from it."

Lo Ming told him that Rose had used her small crystal ball to investigate the future. She had related to Lo Ming that today was hers to make the best of what she could. That's why she had the Ruby Snake Eyes. The visions in the ball had shown her what may happen. It was up to her on how she would react to the fate it had shown. She told me to reassure you that she would be back. She gave me her necklace with the clear white crystal. If the crystal turns purple, she is well. If it turns black, she will not be back. Handing the necklace to Nick, Lo Ming gave him a kiss on his forehead. Lo Ming said, "That is not from me but Rose."

Nick rocked in the old wooden rocking chair. He had put on Roses' necklace and was staring at the white crystal. Nick hoped to see something that would tell him Rose was fine. The old train's whistle blew in the distance. Nick wanted to stay, but he knew he had to go back to his Grandfather in the desert to improve his skills. It would be good to feel the hot desert sun on his face. He remembered what Rose had told him. He must learn and watch. "Patience, she said, was the hardest skill to learn."

June's heart had an empty hole. How could she wait three weeks? One Feather and his white wolf were in The Land of the Eagle Feathers. Did he survive the earthquakes?

June couldn't help him right now. She still had much to learn. Her hawk feathers had been destroyed in the encounter with **the Dark Forces**. She would need more. The Elders and the Great Medicine Man of her tribe had much to teach her and little time to do it. She would need their knowledge to help save The Land of the Eagle Feathers. By saving the land, she was saving One Feather.

For many years, Mary had studied medicine, legends and myths from around the world. She needed to get back to The Land of the Eagle Feathers. If what the Red Woman said was true, her child was alive. For some reason, she felt her child was. It's a feeling only a mother knows. She would find her child. Nothing would stop her from finding him. Her father had much to answer for. She would use him or anyone to get to her son. She would go back to Maine and try to find some answers. There was one thing that she had to do. She had to tell her father that Raven had betrayed him. There was something else she saw. In the shadows, she saw her stepmother, Benita. They must be working together to destroy David. If David does not get *The Book of Winter*, he would lose his position in the leadership. Losing your leadership in **The Omen** meant death.

Mary realized the world of mysticism, legends and myths was a world all its own. It has its own rules, and you must learn. She needed to see John again. He had answers to her questions. She would get the truth out of him. Hopefully, by reviewing all her diaries and notes again, she would find out something. They were not stored at her house that burned to the ground. She could learn something about him. He is the key to her finding out about everything. Just maybe, she would find out who John really is.

Lo Ming had been out for blood in the fight. She didn't care who or what would try to stop her. She would come back and find a way into The Land of the Eagle Feathers. She loved Moses. She would go back and find Moses' mother. John had said something about that he promised Moses' parents he would protect Moses. Moses's mother knows more. Lo Ming would get the answers.

The old man and his old hound dog were sitting on a porch next to the train station. They asked the old man when the train would arrive. The old man said, "Any time now. By the way, are you short three people?" Antonio replied, "Rose, Moses and John." The old man thought for a while then said, "Well, knowing John and that other two, I think they can take care of themselves. I wouldn't worry too much about them." They started to ask the old man why he thought so. A train whistle sounded. Everyone turned to look at the train arriving. When they turned back to question the old man, he and his dog had disappeared.

The old train came to a halt in front of the loading platform. The conductor in his old black uniform announced, "All aboard." Everyone carried their belongings, climbing up the side metal stairs to the passenger car. Dispersing into the passenger car, each one sat deeply in thought. The old train rumbled down the tracks. It was getting dark. The darkness outside made the windows almost like mirrors.

Looking out the train windows, Mary saw her reflection just for a few seconds. "It didn't look like her. It was someone else from long ago. Mary's father after the Amazon expedition had told her that she was someone special. The Amazon's witch-doctors had given her a gift. Besides saving her life, she was now one of them. What did her father mean by that she thought? She always felt that there was something inside of her that was different after that expedition. She would have dreams about the jungle. There would be witch doctors telling her things about their potions and chants. She just thought that was how her brain had stored the knowledge that she had learned in the Amazon. There was always that feeling that there was more to her than just a professor at a Maine College.

After what she had seen these last few months, she knew one thing, she needed to find some answers. Why had John picked her? There must be something more about her than just she was an expert in medicine and native cultures. He could have picked many more qualified people than her. She also knew she was attracted to John. She had loved several men in her lifetime. Could he be one of them? There was a mystery about him. Everyone has a past. She had more questions than answers. She would be patient. The answers would come at the right time.

The old train pulled into town about 2 a.m. The small town was dark except for one light at the local café. Steam was billowing out from the old engine covering the platform. The conductor in his black uniform took out his gold pocket watch. Looking at it, he called for them to depart the train. He told them that the rest of their baggage would be on the platform. They could get a good meal at the restaurant around the corner.

It had been a pleasure to serve them. They found their baggage in a neat row on the platform. The old train rattled and clanked down the tracks, blowing its whistle three times. Nick thought that's the loneliest sound he ever heard. Walking down to the café, they stopped in to get something to eat. Nobody really wanted to eat. They were just going through the motions.

Inside the café was the old man with his dog. He had been rocking in his rocking chair. He asked them if they were hungry. They looked pretty down about the events of the day. "You got to eat something. It has been a long day for you. A good meal will help you digest what happened today. Even if you don't think it, you did well today. Don't choke on this good food. He got up. Pointing to a large table in the center of the room, he said, "Help yourself."

The table was full of food. There was hot coffee and tea in the cups beside each place setting. The funny thing was that there were exactly the right amount of place settings and the right amount of coffee and teacups. "I'm sure you will find everything to your liking," he said. "Don't worry about paying, it's already been paid for by Mary's father," he said with a twinkle in his eye as he walked out the door. Mary looked a little puzzled but said nothing. Soon everyone was trying to eat. Even though the food was good and needed, nothing could replace the pain of today's events.

The food was what one would call 'good old downhome southern cooking.' Some call it comfort food. They needed all the comfort they could get. Whether it was the food or what the old man put in it, it helped the hurt of not having all of them there. They were missing their comrades. Nick had been through that too many times before. Nick knew that they needed a good laugh. He asked, "Mary, I didn't know your father would be so generous as to buy us a meal." All Mary would say was, "My father isn't known for his generosity. He probably took it as a tax write off." They all laughed. She was probably right. Nick knew that this laughter would break the spell of doom for a little while. It would return when they would be alone. He never liked being alone after a mission. His experience told him that each person will have to find their own way to deal with their demons.

A Native American woman appeared at the café's door. She had been the one with the van that had picked them up before. She said that she would take everyone back to the airport to get tickets back home. Mary told her that she was driving back to Maine. The others said goodbye to her and told her they would see her soon. That's when the Native American woman said, "You mean in three weeks." Everyone had a confused look in their face but said nothing. It was just what it was.

After waving good bye to the others in their black van, Mary went down the old dirt street to get her car from the parking lot. The old man was there with his dog. "I thought you would need your car. I have bad news for you. A bad storm came through here about two days ago. A large branch from that tree over there fell on it. I had to take it to the shop. However, you can use this one," as he pointed to a black 1950 Rolls Royce. "Don't worry, it runs fine. I have a driver to take you back to Maine. He says he knows the way. I have already put your baggage into the trunk," Before she could say anything, he opened the back-passenger door. She got in, not knowing what to say or do. Oh, well, she thought, what else could happen tonight? That's when the window between her and the driver opened. The driver's voice asked, "Should we take the scenic route to get back to Maine? I know you would like that," Startled, she knew that voice. The driver was her father.

"Why are you here, father?" she asked. Her father replied, "Like it or not, I am your father. It would be very upsetting to lose my daughter." "I guess that's the first time I ever heard you say something like that. I didn't think you had that in you," she stated coldly. "You would be surprised to know more. It is another matter that I am here for. My sources say that someone used the **Dark Ones** to attack you. Do you know who?" David asked. "It's more like plural. It was Raven and one that you may not suspect: Benita," she answered.

Mary thought David would be surprised. Her father said, "I had my suspicions. I didn't think they were smart enough to work together. Raven has always wanted me to fail. She wanted to get me out of the way. Raven is dangerous enough by herself. It is your stepmother, Benita, that I worry about the most. I liked Benita for her ambition. The two of them together will be a formidable foe. This book stuff is starting to get complicated. We have many that want to stop us. Don't worry, I will drive you for about four hours. We will need to plan. Failure is not an option for either of us. Benita wants you dead, so she can take over the company. Raven wants me to fail so **The Omen** will get rid of me. They know if I get my hands on *The Book of Winter*, I would be too powerful for anyone to stop including **The Omen**."

Mary asked her father, "Do I have a son? Her father answered, "All in due time, all in due time." Since her father didn't give an answer, Mary got one. Her father would have told her outright if she did not have a son. Mary decided to ask another question to get under her father's skin, "Did you ever love my mother?" Her father answered her back, "Now, that is too complicated to answer. Don't ever ask me that question again!' Mary did get the last laugh. She knew that answer too. They really had told the truth at the stable. She did have a son, and the Red Woman was her mother. She knew her father. It would take someone like him to get her son. She would plan with him. She knew how to play both sides of the fence. If it took her father to get her son back, then she would make a pact with the Devil. She looked at the back of her father's head as he drove, "Now tell me about your plan, I will help you. I never liked my stepmother ever since she tried to kill me."

"There is one thing more," her father stated. "You will need to find out about your past without anyone's help. That is the way it works. I cannot help you. As they say, "It's complicated." Mary didn't care. She would get her son. Both her mother and her father would need to suffer. They had done her wrong. She would have her revenge on both. As June said, "Once a scorpion, always a scorpion."

After they had traveled about four hours, her father stopped the car. "You can take the car from here back to Maine. There's an interesting town near here. It's just up the road. The old man said there was a very good Bed and Breakfast there called Memories. In fact, I had him book you a room. Remember our plan. Our lives depend on it. Her father got out of the car and had Mary take the driver's seat. He walked to an open field. There was a helicopter there waiting for him. She drove off. She was exhausted and needed some sleep.

Mary drove to the next town. It was only ten miles away. It was daybreak. She saw a small diner. She stopped and decided to ask the cook or waitress about where the Bed and Breakfast called Memories was located. The cook covered with tattoos said, "Now, it's an old house that some people say they see unusual things there. That's just a wife's tale, I think." Mary laughed and stated, "Thanks, I don't believe in such stuff, but it sounds interesting anyway. You say it's down the street to the left." "Honey, you can't miss it. It's a three-story house that's red with white trim," he replied.

As Mary opened the restaurant door to leave, she almost ran into a man standing there. She had to blink twice. Standing before her was the old man with his dog. "I hear that you need a place to stay and get some rest before finishing your drive home." he said. "Yes," Mary replied. "My brother called me and wanted me to make sure that you got here alright. He said that he had already made a reservation for you. I know the owner of the house, and she will be glad to see you. If you are ready, you can follow me," he replied to her. Mary went back to her car. She followed the old man and his dog to the Bed and Breakfast. He had an old pickup truck that had more red rust on it than metal.

They arrived at the old house. It took only a few minutes to get there. Mary noticed right away that this house was different from any other on the street. She could sense that there were powers in the house that were new to her. This was going to be interesting.

At the door, they were met by an old gray-haired lady. She politely told Mary she already had a room ready for her. "Just call me Grandy. That's what everyone calls me around here," she whispered to her. Grandy led her up to the second floor to a large green door to the left of the staircase. Opening it, Mary could see that the room looked like a Victorian bedroom. It had a great bed with a wooden frame that was accented with four posts. One probably called this a four-poster bed. The cover was a big quilted blanket that had faces of various people from years ago. The old man sat Mary's things down near the bed. Grandy told her that she had already drawn a hot bath for her in the bathroom. There was fresh soap for her and big towels with other toiletries just for her use. "We will see you later. You need to get some sleep. You look so worn out," she softly said as she closed the door.

Mary couldn't wait to get a hot bath. She needed one. Her muscles ached. She needed the time to think about all that had happened in this past year. A good day's sleep would certainly help that. Taking off her clothes, she carefully lowered herself into the large white Victorian tub. The water was hot but not too hot. She took her time bathing herself with the lovely blue scented soap. Taking a large red towel, she dried herself off. She liked the softness of the towel against her skin. She took a smaller towel and wrapped it around her head.

In the bedroom, Grandy had left some oatmeal cookies and hot tea for a snack. Mary ate a cookie and drank most of the dark black tea. Feeling sleepy, she slipped into bed without putting on any clothes. Her night clothes needed washed anyway. As soon as her head hit the pillow, she fell into a deep sleep. Little did she know that this sleep would change everything; the dreams and images that would come in her sleep had been hidden deep in her subconscious for many years.

She could hear the drum beats coming from the dark green jungle. They were very faint at first and increased in sound slowly. The steady beat pulsated as the sound came nearer. A native medicine man or witch doctor stood beside her lifeless body. She was prone on the ground of the jungle floor. The native medicine man was lighting a sacred fire. Taking a large feather, he would scoop up the sacred smoke and wisp it across her face. She could see all of this clearly. Her spirit was floating above the scene. A white man dressed in jungle guide attire that was muddy and had patches of blood on his shirt stood by the medicine man. Another man approached the scene. He was older, tall and lean with gray hair. She recognized him at once. It was her father. There was an argument between her father and the jungle guide. The guide told her father that he would have not come if he knew it was him that had summoned him. The jungle guide left when her father pulled out a gun.

The jungle drums started beating faster and faster. The sacred fire was growing larger and brighter. She could see that her face was unrecognizable. It was battered and so bruised with much swelling in her cheeks. No one would have been able to recognize her if they had tried. Her father motioned to the medicine man. The medicine man took his feather and pointed to the stars above. Then he touched her face. Her face healed completely. Her father smiled. He patted the medicine man on his back and said, "Nobody will recognize my daughter not even her lover. This accident on the Amazon has been a real blessing."

Mary woke up with sweat flowing down her body. Getting out of bed, she bumped into a full-length mirror as she fell to the floor. She was so weak. As she got up, a reflection caught her eye from the large mirror by her bedside. The reflection was not her but another woman. There were two women in the mirror. Both looked back at her and smiled. They had to be mother and daughter. They were almost twins, but one was just older than the other. The shock of what she saw caused her to faint. She fell into the large poster bed unconscious. The older woman had looked exactly like the Red Woman in The Land of the Eagle Feathers.

Images flowed in Mary's dream. She saw the blanket on her bed raise and the faces looking at her. They were all shouting. Your father killed us. He is evil. All we ever did was try to save the sacred land of our ancestors or help them fight to keep the **Dark Ones** out. Your father wants the secrets of the ages for himself. He wants to exploit the land for its riches. If he gets the secrets, he could destroy everything besides the Land of the Eagle Feathers.

Mary's visions turned to scenes of her growing up. Her father loved her. He could be very hard on her. They would take trips to the wilderness in various parts of the world together. Her father always seemed to be searching for something.

In one scene in a desert, there was a man. He was a guide and somewhat older than her. She could tell that they were in love. Her father objected to their romance. Her father appeared with a gun. He shot her lover. He was bleeding from his wounds. He was dying. She could barely see his face. It was John! Then she recognized the face in the reflection of his eyes. It was the younger woman in the mirror.

The noise of Grandy drawing back the large curtains to let sunlight in awakened Mary. "How long have I been asleep?"

asked Mary. "About 28 hours," replied Grandy. "I got worried about you. The doctor said it was only a slight fever and let you sleep it off. I have a bath awaiting you and some good old home cooked breakfast downstairs," she told her. "Also, I washed and packed your clothes for you. I hope your dreams were not too unpleasant," she stated as she left the room to go downstairs. Her mind started to wander to John. Did he survive in the forest? If he did, how did he? He had to survive. She had a lot of questions for him. She didn't know how to react to him if he did survive.

Deep into the forest, I was following Raven and her bodyguards. I was very careful to be as silent as possible. My thoughts returned to the others. I was a little worried that I should have stayed with them instead of going after Raven. After I heard the loud explosion, I knew that Rose had used the Ruby Snake Eye to finish the fight with the **Dark Ones**. This meant the others probably survived the battle. I wondered where the Ruby Snake Eye had taken Rose and the **Dark Ones**. It would take them to another dimension. If Rose had anything to do with it, it would be one of hers. Rose was powerful. She could take them anywhere. She was a lot like her mother who was a powerful Voodoo Priestess. I kind of felt sorry for the **Dark Ones'** warriors. Rose would win.

Darkness had covered the land when I finally found Raven's camp. It was a good camp with a defensive layout. There were large boulders that encircled it. A firepit was in the middle of it. Tents encircled the firepit. I could see four guards covering each direction. Raven was not making any mistakes. She had taken extra precautions. It would be difficult to get to her.

Something was very wrong about this. My intuition told me that this had been too easy. She had left the fight too soon. She had let me see her. She knew I couldn't pass up an opportunity to get her. She knew I would follow her and try to kill her.

Raven had led me into a trap. I cursed myself for letting my anger get the best of me.

I backtracked carefully a few steps. I saw some thick underbrush to the left of the trail. I took my hands and brushed back the weeds and stepped into the middle of it. I moved the brush and weeds back to look like nobody had disturbed it. I would wait to see what was going to happen.

A dark shadow moved toward me. It looked like a female form. There were two shiny objects in both hands. I heard a voice whisper my name. "John, come out of there. Raven's men are waiting for you to come out in the morning. We need to get down the trail to safety. They are all around us. Forget about her, there will be other times for her." I knew that voice at once. It was Shanna. Why was she here?

"I know what you are thinking. I am here because David sent me and Angela to tell you that you might be ambushed. Well, I guess, we are a little late," Shanna whispered. "Where is Angela?" I asked. "I don't know. She went on to The Land of the Eagle Feathers to try to warn you. I would think more like to warn Antonio, two days ago. I think she is still in The Land of the Eagle Feathers. I am worried about her. I heard loud explosions. She has not come back," said Shanna.

Shanna spun around and threw her two knives at a figure behind her. The figure fell to the ground. I jumped out of my hiding place and ran. Shanna followed me down the trail. There were ten **Dark Ones** behind us. We dodged trees and boulders as we ran down the hillside. Shanna turned and threw another knife, and another **Dark One** fell. I told her to stop throwing her knifes. I would lead them to a trap I was going to set for Raven.

After about a mile, we turned off the trail into a large thicket of thorn bushes. Instead of going through the bushes, we turned just to the left. I pulled Shanna down with me into a small pit that I had covered with brush. We hid ourselves just in time as the **Dark Ones** ran straight into the thorn bushes. Immediately, they started screaming as the thorns tore into their skin. The more they tried to move the thorn limbs, the more they became entangled. Soon, they could not move. We got up from our hiding place. I went up to a man that looked like the leader. "Tell Raven, better luck next time. Until we meet again gentlemen, have a good night!" Shanna couldn't help but laugh. Now, it was time to go to Houston.

Rose was still in trouble. She had at least twenty or more **Dark Ones** on horses behind her. She had taken them into another dimension that she knew well. In this dimension, magic and mysticism reigned. The dimension looked like one that you would picture in books about fairies and goblins. The woods and forests were thick and green with many brooks and small streams with waterfalls. Green moss grew on the rocks and ground. It was like a carpet.

The **Dark Ones** were still chasing her down a trail farther into a dark forest. Her red horse was too fast for them to get very close to her. Their horses were slowed by the heavy armor of the riders. It was easy for her to lose them in in the dark forest.

Her horse moved silently into the forest. She found the small village in a clearing. This was what she was looking for. A few of her old friends ran up to her. They were small and friendly people. The men were about four feet tall. Some of them had full beards. They wore green short pants with shirts that had colorful pictures of flowers on them. The women, a little shorter than the men, had on full loose red dresses with white trim. Everyone had on dark brown six- inch boots.

Yoman asked, "Why are you here?" Rose answered, "I need your help. I have twenty or more warriors trying to kill me. I decided to take them here. I know you are some of the best fighters. You once said that if I ever needed help you would. Let's say that you can repay me for the help I gave you with that evil king that once ruled this land." Yoman smiled, "We would have helped you anyway. You know we love a good fight. It will be an honor to assist you. You must be tired from your journey here. We will have a feast tonight in your honor. We will take care of your little problem tomorrow. First, let's look into the well and see where they are located in the forest."

Rose got off her horse and followed Yoman to a well that had a small roof covering over it. She took out a small gold coin from her money pouch. She threw it into the well. She asked, "Where are the **Dark Ones**?" A low-pitched voice of an old man answered, "About ten miles from here. They are setting up camp for the night. They look like they will not be going any farther tonight. You will be safe until morning."

Yoman gave orders for his men to get their weapons ready. He told them after that to help the women with the feast. Rose loved these people. They loved her. Tonight's feast would be special. She would enjoy being with them one more time. She didn't worry about the **Dark Ones**.

Morning came too soon. Rose had eaten too much and drank too much sweet wine. She bathed in a nearby stream. Her clothes had been cleaned and put out near her bed. After breakfast, Yoman had his warriors ready for battle. There were about 20 of them. They carried small swords and spears. It was what was in their pockets that would do the most damage. They had exploding crystals as well.

It was a simple plan. Rose would let the **Dark Ones** follow her. She would lead them into an ambush. Yoman's men would finish them. Their horses would be the prize for his warriors.

They set up the ambush about a mile from the Dark Ones' camp. Rose rode up to their camp and shouted insults at them. Immediately, the Dark Ones mounted their horses and chased her. She led them to the small canyon where Yoman was waiting. The battle was short.

The only problem was that the **Dark Ones' leader** made it through. He was still chasing Rose. Whatever Rose tried, she could not shake him. He was a great rider. Rose had to slow down because a tree blocked the trail. This gave the leader time to catch up and knock her off her horse.

The Leader jumped off his horse. He picked her up and threw her on the ground. When he was about to cut her with his sword, Rose told him that she had some gold. He could have it if he would let her go. "There's a gold snake charm on my neck. You can have it." She pointed to it. The leader couldn't help himself but look when Rose unbuttoned her blouse to show him. "I will take that, and then you will die," he said. He held his sword blade next to Rose's neck. Rose grinned at him. He pulled the gold snake charm and the golden chain from her neck. The smile on his face turned into a frown. The golden snake charm in his hand started to move. It wrapped around his arm. It was a live rattlesnake. It bit him. He died instantly, falling to the ground. Rose remembered when Nick had given it to her. He said that it was old Apache Indian charm to protect her. She was only to use it when nothing else could help her.

Yoman and his friends buried the soldiers in the dark forest. They kept their horses. Rose would have to stay in this land until the moon was full and bright in the middle of the night's sky. That would be in about three weeks. There would be a ceremony of the moon that would take her and her horse back to her world. Rose needed some time to heal. Her left arm had a deep cut in it. She needed time to reflect. She had many decisions to make before she returned.

Chapter VI
Back home again:
What is happening?

Antonio had arrived in Houston. He would have to go to David's Corporate Headquarters and give a report about The Land of the Eagle Feathers. He had done that the last time he visited the land to David's Board of Directors. This time it is going to be different. David now knew that Angela and Antonia were working together. Antonio had to be careful about how he would play this. He didn't know what game plan David had. Everyone was playing everyone. One thing was for sure. He couldn't trust David. David did have one weakness. David loved power. Whatever David thought of him, he knew that David needed him. David would keep him around until he got *The Book of Winter*.

Antonio was picked up at the airport. He was taken to the hotel where Angela had her apartment. The driver told him that Angela was out of town. She wanted him to stay at her apartment until she got back. The blue suited Bellman opened the car's door. He took Antonio straight to Angela's apartment. He told Antonio that he had already had room service fix him his favorite meal.

Antonio was very disappointed. He longed to see Angela. He needed her for many reasons. He was hoping that they could plan their next move in dealing with David. He was running blind. He needed information about what was going on with the Corporation. He would have to play this by ear. He didn't have all the information he needed.

Antonio realized as he entered Angela's apartment that there was something else bothering him. He had made it a rule not to get too involved with any woman. He could smell the lingering scent of Angela's perfume. He needed Angela more than just a business partner. He missed her. She was getting to him just like many years ago in Rome.

As Antonio sat down at the dining room table, he reflected on what he needed to do. He would need to meet with David and discuss how to handle this new situation. He would have to arrange with the museum a place to decipher *The Book of Summer*. He would use the same cover as before. He would need to get the passages to other members of his group. Nick would be at his grandparents' home in the Southwest desert. Lo Ming would be in San Francisco at her place of business and home. June would be on the Great Plains. Mary would be in Maine at her apartment in the college. Where to send the other passages that he would decipher for Moses and Rose would be anyone's guess. He would not worry. It was up to the Native American woman to deliver them. He would decipher them. It would be up to her to deliver them as she did with passages of *The Book of Spring.*

David was at his office. It had been two days since he had arrived back from his drive with Mary. Antonio had called him to arrange a time for them to meet. He put off Antonio. He told him that he would meet him as soon as Angela got back from her business trip. Antonio didn't mind that too much. This gave him time to start deciphering *The Book of Summer*. Besides, he wasn't in a hurry to talk to David. He hoped to see Angela before he met with David. Antonio was not happy. It was not like Angela not to contact him. Something had to be wrong. She should have contacted him.

It was about midnight when there was a knock on David's office door. He wondered who it could be. Nobody was allowed in the building this late. How could anyone get past the security guards, let alone get through the security alarms of his outer office?

He looked at his security monitor. There was a woman dressed in a tight black jumpsuit standing at his door. Her auburn hair gave her away at once. He opened his door. He knew who would be on the other side of the door. It was Shanna. "Come on in. I have been expecting you. Where is Angela?" he asked. Shanna sat down in the black leather chair by his desk. "This could take a while to explain that part of our trip you sent us on. I will explain what happened later. I can only tell you that I think she is trapped in The Land of the Eagle Feathers?" she answered him back.

David sat back on his leather chair and brushed back his dark black hair. Shanna could see that he was trying to digest this information. She knew what he was thinking. How did Angela get into The Land of the Eagle Feathers in the first place, and how did she get stuck there?

"John sent me to tell you what has happened. I will tell you everything I know. Then I will leave and go to see Nick. He will need me. We lost Rose in the process of fighting your Dark Ones! I don't like being double-crossed. You have some explaining to do as well. It is going to be a long night. We have plenty of time to discuss this. I disabled all the alarms. It is just me and you here. Let's get started. I will tell you something, and you will tell me something. I think that is fair. Don't you?" she stated back to David.

David had to admire Shanna's courage. Not too many people would have the nerve to talk to him like her. Shanna said, "Angela and I decided to split up when we got to the Eagle Train Station. She said that she was going to go to where she thought that the main entrance to The Land of the Eagle Feathers was located. She asked me to go to the hot springs up the trail about a day's ride. She left me there to wait for her to return. That is the last I saw of her. When she didn't show up in two days, I decided to track her to find her. It was easy to follow her trail. I lost her tracks when they stopped at a high plateau. It seems that she went into the mountain. There must have been some kind of passageway to enter The Land of the Eagle Feathers, I couldn't find it.

I wonder, why was she able to get into The Land of the Eagle Feathers when others are not allowed. Later, I heard several explosions on the other side of the mountain. Fearing a mountain slide, I went back down the trail to the Eagle Train Station. While I was there, I saw a small army of **Dark Ones** arrive at the Station. I hid and let them pass. Now, it is your turn to explain why they were there," said Shanna.

David wasted no time in replying. "I suspected that someone had authorized an attack on John's group. As anyone in my position, I have enemies. Some of my enemies are outside my organization, and some are in my organization. There are members that feel that The Land of the Eagle Feathers has enough riches such as: gold, natural resources and rare jewels to satisfy them. Some of the other members want more such as the power contained in *The Book of Winter*. It appears the group led by Raven does not want to take the chance that John would find the book and stop the **Dark Ones** from obtaining those riches. I certainly don't know how Angela could have gotten into The Land of the Eagle Feathers."

"I know of another two groups that would want to stop anyone from obtaining the book. One is Night Panther's tribe, and the other is a group from South America. They both fear that the power contained in the books are too much for anyone to handle. The South American group would be a problem for you. They are powerful. The **Dark Ones** would have to battle them for The Land of the Eagle Feathers," Shanna added.

"You are right. They have already tried to stop Antonio from deciphering *The Book of Spring*. I fear they will try it again. I will put some of my trusted men to guard him. I know he arrived here a couple of days ago. What happened to Moses, Rose and John?" asked David.

"When I followed the **Dark Ones** up the trail, I saw the battle between John's group and your **Dark Ones**. It looked like about 20 or more **Dark Ones** were going to overtake them when Rose rode in and threw a gemstone. When she threw the gemstone, there was an explosion. The **Dark Ones** and Rose vanished. It appears that Rose took them to another dimension and saved everyone. Moses didn't make it out of The Land of the Eagle Feathers. John said that he got caught in an earthquake when they entered the tunnel to return. I saved John when he went after Raven. He is safe. I don't know where he is," stated Shanna.

David wanted to make sure that Shanna knew that he did not have anything to do with the attack on them. "Would I attack your group if I wanted to get *The Book of Winter* for myself? I need John's group to find it. I also wouldn't want my daughter to get hurt." Shanna replied, "That's what I was thinking. You need us."

David told Shanna, "You need to go before anyone sees you here. I suggest that you go to see Nick. My sources say that you two were once lovers. I also know that people have sent you to kill him once. It appears that you did not get the job done. I have not decided which side or sides you are on in this adventure. If I were John, I wouldn't trust you. I know I don't. That's why I like you. You play everyone against each other. I will give you a warning: you may beat me, or you may beat John. You can't beat both of us. So name your poison: John or me."

Shanna turned to leave, "It may be neither of you or both of you. I have not decided yet. It has been a pleasure to have this conversation with you. I will give you some advice: "Women can be very deadly. You seem to have several after you. I know of at least three or maybe, it is four. Goodnight, David and be careful." Shanna closed the door behind her and left. David thought to himself, "That's a woman I wish was on my side. I will have to offer her something that she can't refuse."

Antonio was getting more worried about Angela. He still hadn't heard from her. He decided to go to David's office to talk to him. He had enough of waiting for him to call him back. It was only a few blocks from the Museum to David's corporate office. He knew that David liked to work late. He got there about 8 p.m. His secretary had gone home. David's bodyguards had called him to tell him that Antonio was in the building. They were a little concerned that Antonio looked upset. David told them to let him come up and not disturb them. He would take care of Antonio.

David opened his office door as Antonio walked into David's outer office. "I thought you would come here. Come in and sit down, I have some good brandy and cigars that we can share," David said in a polite voice. Antonio was a little surprised by David's demeanor. "Yes, that would be nice. I would like to have a short conversation with you. I have some questions about what I am supposed to do. Will we be having a Board of Directors meeting like last time?" Antonio asked.

David motioned for Antonio to sit down. David poured Antonio some very expensive brandy and gave Antonio his choice of cigars from a box on his desk. David took a cigar and lit Antonio's cigar with a match. "You should always use a match. Matches are made of wood and do not use any chemicals like lighters. As far as your question, we will be having a meeting of the directors like the last time. You will act the part as you did before. Make sure that you keep them interested in The Land of the Eagle Feathers' rich resources such as gold and gems. I know you have probably taken some more precious jewels from your last trip. Do like you did last time and throw them on the table. That should get their attention. There is only one thing that we will be missing. Angela will not be there," mentioned David.

"What do you mean that Angela will not be there?" asked Antonio. "Let's say that she has been detained," answered David. "What do you mean by detained?" asked Antonio again. "I have some bad news for both of us. I sent Shanna and Angela to warn your group that someone might be trying to attack you. Shanna told me that Angela might have become trapped in The Land of the Eagle Feathers. I don't know how she could have gotten into the land. Maybe you can tell me, Antonio."

Antonio was stunned. He had thought that Angela may have been able to travel to the land. Angela never told him about her past. He thought it was better to act surprised. "I am surprised if she could. What are we going to do about it?" Antonio exclaimed. "Nothing, we are going to act as if Angela is on a business trip for me. You will do the meeting and secretly work on *The Book of Summer* at the museum. You thought I didn't know about that, did you? That is another thing you can ask Angela about," laughed David. "Another thing, Shanna said that John was fine. She had saved him. Don't worry about Angela, she is a survivor. I do worry about you. I will have some of my trusted men keep an eye on your safety. They will be my trusted men. Now let's finish our cigars and enjoy this fine brandy."

Later that night when Antonio got back to Angela's apartment, he was very worried. David knew too much. Angela was on his mind. He needed her to help him with David. He felt a little pain in his heart. He realized that he missed her more now than ever. He dismissed his distress about Angela. In his dreams that night, he wondered if Angela ever thought of him. She never said anything about their relationship. Did she ever feel anything more? In one of his dreams, she was laughing with David about how foolish Antonio was. Antonio woke with a start. He was covered with sweat. Whose side was

Angela on? This question was bothering him. His life depended on the answer to that question.

The next morning, Antonio went to the museum. The Director asked him if he had finished his novel. Antonio told him that it would take another few months to complete. The Director asked him if he was still the main character of his novel. Naturally, Antonio said that he was. The Director told him to take his time on the novel. The Director never knew that he was deciphering the books from The Land of the Eagle Feathers. Antonio threw himself into deciphering the passages. He knew that they had only a short time to get back to the land. He needed Angela. He just didn't need her. He wanted her. He was addicted to her.

Chapter VII
Love stories:
At what cost?

Nick's grandmother was outside putting clothes on the clothesline to dry. She noticed in the distance some dust. She hoped that it would be Nick traveling on his grandfather's motorcycle. It was about time for him to come back. She put the last of the clothes on the line. Nick would be thirsty for something to drink. She would get him some cool water from the well. Summers were hot in the Southwest deserts of North America. It wasn't long before Nick drove up to their home. She was waiting for him under the shade of the old tree in the front yard.

Nick took off his goggles and motorcycle helmet. His grandmother took one look into his eyes. Like a doctor looking at a patient, she knew that something was wrong. She didn't say anything. Nick would tell her later. She was glad to have him back. She gave him the glass of cool water to drink. "I have some food fixed for you inside," she said. "You will have to tell me how things went."

Nick followed her inside. She had made some tacos out of cornmeal. "I must warn you. I have seasoned these well. They are very hot like your grandfather likes them. He is expecting you. He told me that you would come today. He is down by the Cave of Elders." Nick's grandmother watched Nick wolf down the food. "Grandson, I can feel there is sadness in your heart. Your eyes tell me that someone dear to you is in trouble. When you feel like it, you can tell me. I will be here to listen. You better get going. Your grandfather says that he has much to teach you and a very short time to do it."

Nick replied to his grandmother, "I could never hide anything from you. I will talk to you later." His grandmother saw a tear in Nick's eye. She gave him a hug. "It will be alright. Come to me tonight, and we will talk." Nick took off on his cycle. His grandmother was glad about one thing. At least, Nick wanted to talk about it. When he came home from the war, he never talked about it.

She had started to clean up the kitchen. A woman's voice startled her. "You must be Nick's grandmother." She turned to see Shanna at the front door. "And you must be Shanna. I have been expecting you. Nick will need both of us to get over what has happened. He has lost too many friends." "You mean, we have lost too many friends," Shanna stated. "Yes, both of you have. Maybe, I can help you both. Nick is going to need you. Let's get you something to eat. We have a lot to talk about." Nick's grandmother took Shanna by her arm and led her to the kitchen table. She knew instantly by touching Shanna arm's that Shanna had feelings for Nick. "By the way, how did you know my name?" Shanna asked. "You should know better than ask that. I know that you are in love with my grandson, even if you won't admit it."

It took Nick about four hours to find the Cave of Elders. His grandfather was waiting in the shade of a large boulder. It would be getting dark in a few hours. His grandfather had fixed them some stew for supper. "I know that you will be wanting to go back to spend the night at the house. We have more important business to attend to tonight and tomorrow. "The Elder of the cave sent me visions of what happened to you on your last journey to The Land of the Eagle Feathers. I know of your demons. You cannot run away from them. You must embrace them. You are very fortunate to have people who care for you. After we eat, we will smoke and find you some peace," his grandfather said softly. Nick loved to hear his grandfather's voice. It was like a whisper in the desert wind. You had to listen carefully, or you will miss something important.

Shanna was getting a little restless. She asked Nick's grandmother when Nick would be back. His grandmother said, "He should be here tomorrow evening. It is too late and dangerous to travel at night in the desert. He needs to spend some time with his grandfather and in the Cave of Elders. He is in a very fragile state. There is a spare bedroom for you to spend as much time as you want here. We need to talk about Nick. I need to get to know you better. You need to have someone talk to you. I do not make judgments about people. Let's go on the veranda and talk. I have some desert tea I would like you to try."

The cold desert night was bright with stars. In the distance, a lonely coyote could be heard. Nick felt at peace with this place. They sat near the campfire to stay warm. Nick watched the flames of the fire as they burned the wood. His grandfather said, "Many years ago, it was a custom to smoke the sacred herb and see visions of the past and future. It is time for you to do that to see and embrace the past and future. Tomorrow, you will go into the Cave of Elders by yourself and learn. I will light the sacred pipe. You will smoke the sacred herb. I will be here if you need me. Remember, you cannot change the past. I know you are tormented by leaving those behind. Life and destiny can be a difficult thing to deal with."

His grandfather lit the sacred pipe. He gave it to Nick. Nick took several deep puffs on the pipe. Nick sat back and watched the flames of the fire grow. The visions started to dance in the fire. His friend, Jacob, was standing in front of him. Jacob told him not to worry about him. He was where he was. "I know you wanted to come back for me. It was your duty. Sometimes, duty is not enough. What good would it had been for you to die? I was already dead. You had to save the others. That was more important than me. I am but dust in the sands of time. You will always be my friend."

"Jacob, I loved you like a brother. I could not bear the guilt of leaving you there for the birds and insects to feast on. I should have come back for you," cried Nick to the vision before him.

"Isn't that the circle of life? Nick, you must forgive yourself. I know that you were like a brother to me. Wars are terrible things. You have a chance to save your new friends. You cannot do that with this monkey on your back," Jacob whispered to him. Tears ran down Nick's face. He didn't want his friend to go. Jacob looked back at Nick, "One day, we will be together. You have a destiny to fulfill. I have done my part. I did what I was supposed to do and saved your life. You must do what you are supposed to do." Jacob faded into the darkness of the night.

There were other dreams and visions that Nick had. He saw his father and mother. He saw Shanna and Rose talking about him. He felt love from both of them. He saw a bridge that had two lanes. In one lane at the other side was Rose, and in the other lane at the other side was Shanna. He had to decide which way to go. That was when his grandfather woke him.

"It is time for you to enter the Cave of Elders," his grandfather said.

Nick's grandmother had built a small fire in the fireplace on the veranda. Shanna sat down next to her. "It's very peaceful in the desert at night," Nick's grandmother began. "You know how I knew you would come. I saw a vision of you and Nick last Spring. You were together. I could feel that you both cared deeply for each other. You risked your life for him. You saved him once from his demons in another desert far away. He was a lonely boy when he was young. His parents were always on some journey or mission to faraway lands. He didn't have many friends. He loved to journey into the desert."

"You are much like him. Your mother and father died when you were very young. He wrote to me once about a girl he met in high school. He said for the first time he was happy. He said he never loved a girl so much. She was just like him. They would go to the beach and talk. He said that they really didn't have to talk. They communicated with their thoughts. You know who she was, don't you?" Shanna answered, "That was a long time ago. I was very young. I never had been in love. I was scared to love anyone. Everyone that I loved before died. I couldn't take that chance with Nick. I ran away from him."

"Nick wrote me another letter. He was lost. He said that his girl had left him. He didn't know what to do. He did find a friend. His name was Jacob. Here is a picture of Jacob in his army uniform." Shanna took the picture and moved it close to the fire to see it better. The man in the picture looked very familiar to Shanna. "He does look like Moses, doesn't he? That is why you must help him. Nick has feelings for another woman. It is hard enough to lose one friend. I don't have to say anymore. He may lose her to someone else. He cannot lose Moses. He would never forgive himself. That is why you are here. It is both your destinies to be here. Make the most of it. Don't have any regrets of what you do! You must be patient.

Nick will be back tomorrow night. I trust you will help him. It is time for us to get some sleep. You have much to think about."

As Shanna got up to go to her room, Nick's grandmother smiled at her. Shanna had not cried for many years. She thought she was too tough for that. Nick's grandmother knew more than anyone about Shanna's destiny. It would take many twists and turns. Shanna needed to come back to that little girl on the beach. Shanna needed to let herself feel again. Yes, you do Nick's grandmother thought. They both needed to face their demons.

It was late afternoon when Nick and his grandfather arrived back from the Cave of Elders. Nick appeared to be more relaxed. He saw a black jeep in front of the house. It had an eagle on its hood. He had seen it once before. When he entered the house, his heart jumped. Shanna was there seated at the dinner table by his grandmother. They were talking to each other like old friends. "I have an old friend of yours. She said she wanted to check on you. She says her name is Shanna. I think you once had a girlfriend named that," his grandmother gave him a devilish grin.

Nick looked at Shanna. She looked like that young girl he had known so long ago. It was if time had stopped. Her auburn hair was in pigtails. Her dark skin was tanned by the sun. Her short cut-offs and shirt tied at her waist took him back to his high school days. "Now, it isn't nice to stare. I know she is pretty. She said that someone named John wanted her to spend a couple of days with you. He is worried about you. Don't worry about John. Shanna saved him. I have fixed supper for you. Let's eat," announced his grandmother. Nick's grandmother may have looked happy to have Shanna here. His grandfather was not so sure.

After the evening meal, everyone went to the veranda to have some wine. It was a lovely night with the stars bright and a full moon. Nick's grandparents excused themselves after about an hour of small talk. They said that they were tired and needed some sleep. That left Nick and Shanna alone. There is a legend about a desert night like this. It says that it has a magic all its own. Shanna had removed her pigtails and let her hair fall around her shoulders. Shanna looked at Nick. In the moonlight, he reminded her of the boy she knew long ago.

Nick asked Shanna if she would want to go on a moonlight walk in the desert. Shanna said that would be lovely. They got up and started to walk down the dusty road. Nick said he knew of a good spot that overlooked the desert valley. Nick had picked up a blanket if the night got too cold. They walked for a while talking about old times. The magic of the moonlight was working. When they came to a certain place on top of a hill, Nick spread the blanket down on the ground. They laid back to look at the stars and valley below. Nick couldn't help himself. He felt like a young teenager again. He kissed Shanna on her lips. She couldn't help herself. She kissed him back. The moon seemed to move around the sky. They were on that beach again. They took their time making love.

It was about dawn when they arrived back at the house. Shanna said. "It was nice. I will be leaving tomorrow. You have nothing to be sorry for. I do not want to get between Rose and you. Rose is a big girl. She can take care of herself. I will always remember that summer at the beach. Learn all you can from your grandparents. We will need it to get the others back. Good bye for now. I will see you again at the Eagle Train Station. I have finished my business here. I have unfinished business elsewhere."

Shanna ran into the house. She didn't want Nick to see the tears flowing down her face. Shanna left that night before Nick got up. She still had tears in her eyes. Her heart was in pain. It was the first time she had felt this way for a long time. The next three weeks would be the longest three weeks of her life.

Nick missed Shanna the moment he realized she was gone. She was right. They would always have that summer at the beach. A tear formed in his eye as he thought of Shanna. He was at peace. He would learn all he could from his grandparents. He would save his friends. He would see them again. He would see Shanna and Rose again. He needed to see Rose. His heart was heavy. Rose was the new love in his life, but Shanna was the old love. His mind turned to the dream. He was at the bridge. Which lane would he choose? He didn't know. He would leave it up to destiny.

Nick went over to his motorcycle. On it was a note from Shanna: "I needed to tell you one more thing. John is alive. I saved him from the **Dark Ones**. I don't know where he is. He just left on his horse at the Eagle Train Station. He had said something to the old man with that old hound dog. He got on his white horse and galloped down the train tracks. I never saw him again."

This should have helped Nick, but all it did was bring up issues. He was worried about Moses, John, One Feather and Rose. Visions of Rose and her laugher filled his mind. She had helped him so much. She had taught him to live again. Did she survive? She had told him that she would be back before she exploded the crystal. Did she make it? He would only know when he would get back to the Eagle Train Station. His heart was breaking for his friends. He knew one thing as tears filled his eyes. He was never going to leave them behind.

June was not in a good mood. It had taken her two days to get to her tribe on the Great Plains. She was worried about One Feather. The anxiety of not knowing what happened in The Land of the Eagle Feathers was playing with her mind. There was not one sign that he was alright. Being a spirit warrior, he should have been able to contact her in some way. Midnight, her black wolf, was showing signs of depression. Midnight would only lie down and look up with her sad eyes. She would not eat. June could tell that she missed Snow, One Feather's white male wolf.

June went to her tribe's great medicine man. He was known for his wise ways. White Hawk told her to go to the tribe's ceremonial site to say her prayers to the Great Creator for their safe return. She needed to perform the prayer ceremony to ensure that the Great Creator would hear her prayers.

When she arrived at the ceremonial site, she looked for the great prayer circle. She found it without any trouble. She took off her moccasins as a sign of respect for the Great Spirit.   She lit the prayer fire made of Cedar wood in the center of the prayer circle.   Cedar is the most sacred of wood because it carries its leaves all year long. Taking out one hawk feather for her prayer feather to symbolize One Feather, she placed it in her right hand. She started swaying and looked up to the sky with both arms raised to the sky with her prayer feather pointing to the sky. She song her prayer song called *Listen to the Voice of Love.* Her voice is soft as her prayer song flowed from her breaking heart.

Oh, Great Creator, One so high
Oh, Mother Earth, Father Sky
Hear my prayer sent to above
Listen to the voice of love

I humbly ask you to see
This prayer is not for me
I pray to you in One Feather's name
I beg you, I have no shame

Please protect him, allow him to live
My prayer is all I have to give
This pain cuts like a knife
To save him, I offer you my life

I raise my arms, and beg for mercy
Send down your powers and let it be
Without him, the river ceases to flow
My life is done, I am ready to go

Hear my prayer, and let me know
He's safe before I go
Before I fly to the skies above
Listen to the voice of love

June sat down in the circle to await a sign. She noticed a Morning Dove in the sky. A large hawk is flying to catch it. Her wolf sat down beside her. The large hawk instead of killing the Morning Dove touches its wings. The large hawk becomes a Morning Dove. They fly high up into the sky together. June felt a great relief come over her. It was a good sign.

Midnight, her wolf stood up. Next to her a Great Medicine Man appeared. It was the one on the sacred mountain. His name is Red Bear. "I know that you are trying to call out to your love. I have come to challenge you for his life. You can save him and yourself if you give up your quest for the Great Books of The Land of the Eagle Feathers," he commanded her.

June looked at the Great Medicine man, Red Bear. "I would rather die first. One Feather is an honorable brave. He would say the same," she replied. Red Bear started to point his rattle at her. Before he could do or say anything, White Hawk, the Great Medicine Man of June's tribe, appeared in the sky above. White Hawk said, "Red Bear, you are not a warrior because June is not your equal. She is like a young bird with a broken wing. You must deal with someone of your same stature to be worthy of a challenge. I will take her challenge for her. You know that I am a worthy foe for you." "I have no quarrel with you, White Hawk," Red Bear replied. "I know that you don't know of June's powers. She is more than a worthy foe for me. She is capable of stopping me." "That may be, Red Bear but not today. She came here to pray for her love. This is sacred ground. Go, before I forget that it is a sacred place," shouted White Hawk. In a puff of red smoke, Red Bear was gone.

White Hawk looked at June and said, "You are a great medicine woman but do not challenge someone like Red Bear. He will fight to the death. He knew you had been weakened by the loss of your love. Take the sign of the Morning Dove to heart that the Great Creator sent you. Go back and take your wolf with you. Your quest is not over. You have much to do. Your grandfather has much to teach you if you are going to survive the next journey." White Hawk turned into a great white hawk and flew high into the sky. June took her wolf and headed to her grandfather's home.

June's heart ached for One Feather. Her heart also ached for Moses, Rose and John. At that moment, she knew she had to survive to return to The Land of the Eagle Feathers. Tears flowed down her face. She wanted to be home with One Feather in The Land of the Eagle Feathers. She had to hope that the sign was one of One Feather surviving. There would be many lonely nights ahead where she would cry for his safe return. Midnight would join her misery with her lonely howl every dark night for her mate, Snow, to come for her.

Mary was bewildered about what she saw last night. She decided to go back to Houston. Her father had a meeting scheduled with his Board of Directors. She would attend. If she didn't attend, the Board would wonder why she wasn't there. It would be difficult on how to handle Raven and Benita. Her father would know what to do about them. She had several questions to ask him. The Board Meeting would be the important thing. She hoped that Raven and Benita did not see her during the fighting. Mary was upset and mad at the whole situation. Whoever took her child should have to pay. If the

Red Woman really was her mother, why did she take her child? The more she thought about her child, the more upset she got. She was upset that she must have missed at least 11 years of his life. She would never have the opportunity of watching him grow up. She would have missed her chance to be a mother. Sadness was overcoming her as she drove down to Houston. She remembered the boy that played the flute at the Council Meeting. His face kept appearing in her mind. She didn't have to guess. The boy had to be her son.

Mary didn't care what it would take. She would go back to The Land of the Eagle Feathers. Nobody would stop her. She would confront the Red Woman. The Red Woman would have to explain herself. Any interference by Raven or Benita would be the end of them. She would not bat an eye to take them out. She could be as cold as they were.

After about two hours of driving toward Houston, Mary pulled into a rest stop. She looked over at the car parked beside her. In the car was a mother with her small child, that was too much for Mary. She had held it in too long. Tears flowed down her face, she put her two hands on her face and cried. She had not cried for years. After a while, a State Police Officer knocked on her car window. She tried to dry her tears as she rolled down her car window. "Is anything the matter?" asked the State Police Officer. "No, I am just happy to hear that my son is well and doing fine," replied Mary. "Why is that," the female officer asked. "He had been lost, but now he has been found. I just got the news. I am going to Houston to see my father about him. Thanks for asking," answered Mary. "No problem," said the police officer, "Be careful, it's a long drive to Houston." Mary nodded yes to her.

Mary knew that she wouldn't be able to make it to Houston until late tomorrow. She pulled into a good hotel off the interstate. She hadn't realized how tired she was until she got to her room. It had a queen bed. She dropped her luggage.

The bed was inviting her. She thought she would lay down in the bed before getting something to eat at the hotel's restaurant. As she got comfortable, she fell into a deep sleep.

The dreams returned. Many scenes of her father and mother flowed in and out of her dreams. None of them made sense. She found herself on the mountain ridge top of Eagle Mountain. In front of her was the young boy with his flute. The Land of the Eagle Feathers started to shake and roll. Huge boulders fell and moved back and forth. The boy started to cry out to her, "Mommy, come help me! I need you! I am scared! Please come back to me!"

Mary woke up from her dream. She had been crying for her son. She had to get back to The Land of the Eagle Feathers. Not only was she crying for her son, she realized that she was crying for the others that had been lost: Moses, Rose, John and One Feather. Did they survive? There was one other thing. When she had thought of her son's father, she saw a face. That face shocked her. It was John.

She was confused. She had to get back to The Land of the Eagle Feathers. She had to find her son. She had done the one thing that she thought impossible. She had begun to care for the others. Her heart was breaking as she cried like never before.

Antonio had deciphered several of the messages. He was having difficulty in concentrating on which passages to choose. In *The Book of Spring*, it seemed easy to find the passages with the clues to finding *The Book of Summer*. His mind kept returning to Angela. Maybe, this was what was bothering him. Not only did his heart ache for her, but his whole body did. His thoughts would go back to when they first met in Rome over twenty years ago. He had been assigned by The Council of Religions to find a secret cult of evil ex-priests and eliminate them. Angela happened to be one of the top cult members' bodyguards. He still remembered what she wore when he first saw her.

He had used her to get into the cult's headquarters. He used the idea of him asking her out on a date to find out information. He had not counted on getting involved in a relationship. They became lovers. When he eliminated the whole sect of priests, he made sure that Angela had been detained by the police on a bogus charge. He never saw her again until he was assigned by the Council about a problem with The Land of the Eagle Feathers.

He didn't want this job. After he did some checking, he changed his mind. By now, both Angela and he had gotten a reputation that they would do anything for the right amount of money. He made sure he would answer her advertisement for a man that could decipher any ancient language. Angela seemed happy when he answered her ad. When they got together, it didn't take long for them to decide to hatch a plan to take the books for themselves. They both wanted to get even with their bosses. They both wanted to be rich. They both were scorpions. They both wouldn't admit it. They both enjoyed renewing their relationship.

Rico, the Director, had noticed a change in Antonio. Antonio used to have a smile on this face when he was working on his romance novel. Rico had used Antonio in the past to help him find several artifacts. Antonio and Rico got along very well. Antonio had told him that he was writing a romance novel based on Rico's love life. This was Antonio's cover for getting Rico to let him use an office in the museum. Rico didn't know anything about the books that Antonio was actually working on.

One day Rico asked Antonio what was wrong. Caught off guard, Antonio didn't know what to say. "What do you mean?" asked Antonio. "You don't seem to be focusing on your work. You have a look of something bothering you," stated Rico. "Well, I am having trouble concentrating," replied Antonio. Rico laughed. "I know what it is that is troubling you, Antonio." Antonio asked, "What?" Rico motioned for Antonio to come into his office. "I know this is personal. This is between you and me." Rico whispered to him. "Please sit down." Antonio took a seat on the antique leather chair by Rico's desk.

"I have known you for several years. We had done a lot of business together. Some of our business was questionable in nature. We have always spoken pretty bluntly. Being another Italian like you, it is our nature to be romantic. Sometimes a romantic author does not recognize the same in their own life. From my vast romantic adventures, I know the answer to your problem," stated Rico with a smile.

"Well, Mr. Rico, since you are so smart, you must tell your old friend." Antonio sarcastically half-heartedly replied. "It is simple. Antonio, you have all the symptoms," Rico stated like he was some medical doctor. "What symptoms are you talking about? Antonio asked. "You are in love. You miss her. I did some checking, and my source says you are staying at a beautiful exotic woman's apartment. It is said that she is on a business trip and isn't home. It does not take a genius to figure out you miss her. Since you can't concentrate, I would say that you love her. That is what one Italian to another Italian would know."

Antonio sat back for a while. Rico took out a bottle of Italian wine from his desk. "Shall we drink to beautiful women and love. It's too bad that we can't love them all. Believe me, I have tried. She must be very special to catch you in her spell." Antonio took one of Rico's glasses. Rico filled it with wine. "You are so right. She does know how to cast a spell," Antonio replied. Little did Rico know that Antonio was wondering if Angela could cast such a love spell to make sure he kept coming back to her.

Antonio was sure of one thing. Rico did have good sources. To know this much about him, Rico might be more than Rico seemed. Another thing he was sure of was that Rico was right.

He did miss Angela more than he wanted to admit. Love was something that hurt and clouded one's mind. Of all the women he had been with throughout the years, only Angela had gotten to him. Rico was right. He must love Angela. He couldn't wait to get to The Land of the Eagle Feathers. He had to know if Angela was playing him. If she was, it would break his heart. He remembered those many years ago when he had to leave her in Rome. A tear formed in his right eye. Rico noticed. Rico just shook his head and said, "Drink up. We have several bottles to drink tonight."

Antonio woke up with a terrible hangover. He was in Angela's bed in her apartment. He reached over to touch her. He soon remembered that she was gone. In his dreams last night, he saw her. It appeared that she was crying. Were the dreams real, or just dreams? Was she trying to reach out to him? He only hoped that was true. Missing her was killing him like a slow poison. If he didn't see her soon, he would be no use to anyone.

Antonio got up and dressed. He went straight to the museum. To his surprise, he ran into Rico. Rico was shocked Antonio had come in to work. "Are you okay, Antonio?" Rico asked. Antonio replied, "This is the best I have felt in years. I can see clearly now. I can't wait to finish my writings. I know the next passages of our book and who to send them to for them to proof. It won't be long for me to finish the part of our novel about the season I call Fall." Rico was somewhat confused about what Fall had to do with the novel.

Antonio was worried about the missing members of his group. What had happened to Moses, John, One Feather and Rose? What had happened to The Land of the Eagle Feathers? He was worried about all of these things. Most of all, he was worried about Angela. Antonio was not a patient man. Waiting to return to The Land of the Eagle Feathers was against his grain. He had to do something. What was he going to do with the passages that belong to Moses and Rose? The only thing that he could do was finish the passages and send them to the other members. That would keep him busy for a while. He also had to attend the Corporate Meeting next week.

To answer some of these questions, he had to find John. John was a survivor like Angela. Antonio was becoming more upset with himself. Why was he so concerned about the members of his group? He had taught himself to not become attached to anyone. It was not good for business. It could also get you killed.

Time was standing still, and it was also running out. The only answers were in The Land of the Eagle Feathers. He was going back with or without all the members. He had to find out his destiny. Then, it hit him. He had to find out about all their destinies. They were all tied together like the famous knot that Alexander the Great had to solve before becoming the greatest conqueror of all.

Lo Ming had returned to San Francisco. She went directly to her business. Her business partner, Van Lo Sing, was in his office examining the accounts. His graying hair and white shirt with rolled up sleeves gave him a very distinguished appearance. Lo Ming noticed that there were many packages ready for shipment to the Far East. "I think I did the right thing by making you a full partner. It looks like business has never been greater," she said to him. "Well, you could at least say, "Hello," before you got to work on our business," Van Lo Sing wickedly smiled. "No, I didn't come here for that. I came for some advice. Something has been bothering me. I need some advice on how to handle it," asked Lo Ming.

"Now, we are in the antique and artifact business, not the psychology business. However, for you I will make an exception," said Van Lo. "I suggest that we talk about it later at dinner tonight to cerebrate you coming home about 8 o'clock at my place." "That's a date. See you tonight. I better get home and change into something more presentable," Lo Ming said on her way out.

Lo Ming arrived at her home in the hills in a short time. She opened her door and put up her suitcase. It felt good to be home. She couldn't wait to take a nice hot shower. It would be about three hours before she had to leave to get to Van Lo Sing's home. She sat down on her bed. She was trying very hard to hold it together. She missed Moses. She wondered if he would ever forgive her. Her nerves were at a breaking point. She needed to meditate. Instead of a shower, she would take a long hot bath with her special mixture of flowers and scented oils.

It wasn't long before she slowly lowered herself down into the large bathtub. It felt so good to be home. The mixture of exotic flowers and oils soon had the soothing effect and healing effect she needed. She hadn't realized that she had been so beat up by the fight in the forest. She had bruises on bruises on her shoulder and back. Lying back, she let the mixture work on her body. It wasn't long before she fell asleep.

The dreams came back to Lo Ming. She was in the tunnel entrance to The Land of the Eagle Feathers. The earth was trembling, and dust was everywhere. Moses has barely got into the entrance. Lo Ming could not help herself. She had to save Moses from his fate. Taking a step forward, she took her fighting stick and pushed against Moses' muscular chest. She could not get it out of her mind. It was the look on his face as he fell outside of the tunnel. She would always remember the disbelief on his face as he fell outside. The rocks covered the opening to the tunnel before he could get up. The last she saw of him was him running down into the valley dodging large boulders and deep fiery pits forming in the ground around him.

Lo Ming woke up in a start. This had been her dream every night for the last several days. She looked at the clock in the bedroom. It was almost 7 o'clock. She had to get dressed and hurry to be in time for the Van Lo dinner.

Lo Ming drove very fast to get to Van Lo Sing's home in time. She didn't notice a red sports car following her. Van Lo met Lo Ming at his door. "Come in and let's have some wine while the dinner is finishing in the oven," said Van Lo. Van Lo knew how to entertain quests. The wine and dinner that followed was fit for royalty. Afterwards, he invited her to have some tea on his back patio.

Van Lo didn't waste any time. He asked, "What is bothering you? You were not yourself at dinner. I know it wasn't my cooking. I am a master chef. I feel that you want to talk about something. I think that something has to do with your friend or should I say lover: Moses."

Lo Ming opened up to Van Lo, "It has to do with a lot of things. I have been keeping some things from Moses. I didn't know how to tell him. It has to do with his mother, father and me. I had a meeting with his mother, and I didn't tell him. His mother came to me shortly before I went back. She wanted me to know about some concerns she had."

"Were the concerns about you and her son?" asked Van Lo. "No, not really. It was more about Moses and his family," Lo Ming replied. "It seems that Moses has a dark side. His mother was worried that he would revenge his father. It seems that Moses will go to extremes to find and get even with anyone that hurts his family. His mother said that he once hunted down ten men that left her and him for dead in the deserts of China. He killed each one of them. It's not that he killed them, it's how he killed them." related Lo Ming.

"That's not too unusual for many men to do," said Van Lo. "It's who he has the need to revenge now. It seems that he blames a friend of his parents for the death of his father. He even blames his mother. They had a big fight about it. She wanted me to try to convince Moses to change his mind."

"I see the problem you have. If you say anything to Moses, he will know you talked to his mother. He will be very embarrassed and hurt that you know about it especially since you never told him right away. He may feel betrayed by you."

"It gets worse because I would never let him get his revenge on the man that Moses hates. His mother made me promise to keep that man safe. That man holds the only hope to bring back his father from The Land of the Dead," cried Lo Ming.

Van Lo Sing sat and didn't reply to Lo Ming for a long time. When he answered her, she was shocked at what she heard. "I know who you are talking about. I would have never thought that you would have ever known about John. Yes, I know about The Land of the Dead. It is in The Land of the Eagle Feathers. I once rode with John many years ago. I know Moses' mother and father. They are very good people. I was there when Moses' father was taken. He made John promise that he would always protect Moses' mother and son. John would never fight Moses. John would never harm Moses. He would die first."

"You mean that you knew about John and The Land of the Eagle Feathers. You never told me," shouted Lo Ming. "First of all, you never told me about who the guide was, and where you were going. It wasn't until you told me the story just now that I put it together," he whispered. "But there is another problem with Moses that you are not telling me, Lo Ming."

"Yes, there are two other things. I can't get it out of my mind that the Moses I know has such a dark side, that he can kill without feelings in such a cruel way. I only know a kind and gentle Moses." "What's the other thing?" asked Van Lo.

"We left Moses behind, and I am the one that left him in The Land of the Eagle Feathers to die. I was trying to save him, but I may have killed him!" cried Lo Ming. Lo Ming went on to tell Van Lo the whole story about what happened.

Van Lo was worried about what to say to Lo Ming. He probably had said too much already. "I can only say one thing to you. You must find Moses's mother and discuss how to handle this problem. She is wise. She has her faults. Like you, she is very independent. She loves Moses very much. She would never forgive herself if she came between you and Moses. Moses is a man of the Outback. The Outback can be very unforgiving. I am sure that you and his mother will find a way to get Moses to understand. We are not always what we seem to be. Moses is basically a good man. You will need to remember that he loves you. If he is like his father, he would die for you. There is one other thing that I have to give to you. Come with me before you go home."

Van Lo went to an old chest that was covered with a Persian rug. He uncovered it and opened it. He took out something and put it into Lo Ming's hand. "It's a blue diamond. All you have to do to summon Moses' mother is to rub it and wish for her to come to you. She knows where you live. She will come. You need to leave and get some rest. You are a lucky woman." Van Lo stated.

"Why is that?" asked Lo Ming. "You have the love of a Bushman. They will love you forever. You also have the ability to bring back Moses' father. The only thing is that you have to keep John alive."

Lo Ming left Van Lo Sing's home confused. She had a lot of things to digest. It would take time to sort things out. She did realize that John had picked her because of her friend, Van Lo Sing. She did do what Van Lo told her to do. She did take out the blue diamond and wish for Moses' mother to come to her. She needed to talk to her. She went to bed. Sleep still didn't come easily.

In the middle of the night, her bedroom door burst open. A tall man was standing there. He had two Chinese swords in his hands. "I hear you are one of the best in the world at martial arts. I have come to find out. I was given a contract to kill you. I will give you a chance to live. If you beat me, you will live. If I win, I will kill you," he proudly stated the challenge to her.

Lo Ming knew who this stranger was. He was considered the best contract killer in the world. Everyone in the underground knew of him. She once saw him in action. He was good. He was better than good at his trade. She smiled back at him, "I'm at a disadvantage, Mr. Omega."

"Don't worry, it will be a fair fight. I want everyone in the world to know that I beat the great Lo Ming on an equal basis. Shall we go outside and finish this, Lo Ming?" Mr. Omega spoke to her with the respect she deserved. "We shall," answered Lo Ming.

Lo Ming's backyard was a large grassy yard. It was flat with a few large boulders for decoration. Mr. Omega tossed her one of his swords. They both nodded to each other in respect for their skill. Not a word was said between them. The fight began. Both sized each other up by striking and moving. Sparks flew as the razor-sharp steel blades struck each other. Mr. Omega was pleased that Lo Ming was a master with the swords. He knew if he beat her, he could get any amount he wanted for his contracts.

Lo Ming fought like a tiger. Several times she thought she had him. Mr. Omega would somehow slice out of her grasp. He attacked her with skill and the grace of a panther about to kill its prey. After about 30 minutes, they both were getting exhausted. Mr. Omega thought that he would not last much longer at this pace. He reached into his pocket and threw some red dust into Lo Ming's eyes. She was blinded for a second. Mr. Omega knocked Lo Ming's sword out of her hands. "I guess this is the end for you, Lo Ming," he laughed. He had his sword at Lo Ming's chest. "I will make this quick for you."

That's when they both heard a voice behind him. "No, Mr. Omega, I will make it quick for you. Turn around and face me or die with your back to me. Either way, I will win," said Moses's mother with Lo Ming's sword in her hands.

Mr. Omega turned around. He started to sweat. He knew that the only one that ever beat him in competition was in front of him. "So, it is you, Li Ching. How did you know I would be here?" Mr. Omega asked. "I heard that a contract had been taken out for Lo Ming. The only one that would ever take such a contract had to be you. I just waited until Lo Ming returned. I have been watching the fight. She had you beat, but you have dishonored yourself by cheating. I will take pleasure in killing you," Moses mother said in a disrespectful manner. Mr. Omega skillfully swung his blade at her. She graceful sidestepped him and jumped over him. Mr. Omega recovered to find a blade at his chest. "You wouldn't kill me in cold blood?' he said. As if to answer that, Li Ching pushed her blade into his heart and said, "You disrespected a challenge. You should die like a coward."

Lo Ming was shocked at what Moses' mother had done. "Don't be so innocent, Lo Ming. Moses and I have had many adventures together. One thing that we understand is that don't leave any enemy around unless you can keep them close. This man would have come back and killed you in due time. He would have come back and killed Moses too. We call it survival. Now tell me what happened in The Land of the Eagle Feathers and leave nothing out. I will tell you how to handle Moses."

Lo Ming told her the whole story including the parts of not telling Moses about her meeting with her. She also told Li Ching about her pushing Moses back into The Land of the Eagle Feathers. Lo Ming was surprised that his mother seemed to take it in stride.

"Lo Ming, my son is alive. He is too stubborn to die without my consent. I will tell you how to handle this situation. When you first see him, don't say anything. Just beat the tar out of

141

him to get his attention. He will have to be on the ground or his temper will get the best of him, and he won't listen to you. Tell him the truth. Tell him everything in your heart and soul. Tell him what happened here tonight. He will be hurt, but he will soon realize that you are more important than anyone. Tell him not to hurt John. He is the only one that can bring back his father. When you are done with that, drag him into your tent and make love to him like there is no tomorrow. I promise you that that will work," Li Ching stated.

"How do you know it will?" asked Lo Ming. "I know, it did for me and his father," smiled Li Ching. "There is one other thing I need to tell you. I will have Van Lo Sing tell everyone about the challenge tonight. He will tell the underworld that you had him beat, but he cheated. He will say that I killed Mr. Omega in a fair fight because he cheated. He will also tell everyone that I will revenge anyone that tries to kill you, and you will do the same for me. That should keep us safe for a time. I must go. You get back and save my son, or I will come back and kick your butt."

Lo Ming watched Li Ching leave. She was alone with her thoughts. She had been consumed by her thoughts about Moses. Other thoughts started flooding in. What happened to Rose, John and One Feather? What happened to the Land of the Eagle Feathers? Would she ever see Moses again? The pain of not knowing was overwhelming. She had to find a way to hold on until she could return to the Land of the Eagle Feathers. This was going to take every ounce of inner strength she had. She would find it. Failure was not an option. She would return to the Land of the Eagle Feathers.

Rose was still stuck in the alternate dimension. This gave her time to reflect on several issues that were bothering her. She often thought of Nick. He was always kind and gentle to her. He had his issues. We all have issues. It wasn't his fault that what he had seen and done during wartime caused many of his problems. Like many veterans, he needed help. He had been lucky to get help in a VA hospital. He should have kept working with them and joining veterans' groups to continually deal with the unresolved issues. That's the problem with anyone that has issues. They think they are cured, but really there's no cure. You need to work on it each day.

She opened the leather pouch on her belt. Pulling out two dog tags, she looked at what was on them. Nick's name, his serial number, blood type and religion were stamped into them. They were in bad shape. It looked like they had been blown up in an explosion. Someone had sent her these before she left for The Land of the Eagle Feathers for the first time they went. There had been a note attached that said bring these with you. You will find out why later.

Nick was more than four things stamped on two pieces of metal. Veterans are more than that. She remembered the first time she saw him on the train. He was so young. He was full of life. At least, that's what he appeared to be. Maybe it was the fortune teller in her or her other heritage, she saw that quickly. His eyes gave him away. When nobody was around, he would have that thousand-mile stare. One thing that he did made her love him was that he never asked or judged her. He always treated her like a lady with respect. He would make funny jokes and say the dearest of words.

Rose's thoughts turned to her other great love. Zan and her had met at the Mardi Gras many years ago in New Orleans. She had just opened her small business. They actually bumped into each other. She was walking in the parade wearing a tight low-cut dress with hundreds of beads hanging down her neck. Zan was a slender tall dark-haired young man. He must have been looking at her beads or more at her ample chest when he ran straight into her. It was obvious what he had been looking at. Most young men could not pass that up. She laughed at him because he had trouble explaining why he didn't watch where he was walking. He told her that he should make up for being so clumsy. He invited her for a drink at a local restaurant that was famous for its food and wine. The rest was history.

They found out that they had much in common. It was when Zan visited her shop that specialized in mystical items and other exotic items that he told her about himself. He was a son of a very powerful wizard. Even though Zan had a natural skill for it, he didn't want to follow in his father's footsteps. Zan wanted to do other things. It turned out that his father blamed Rose for his son not wanting to follow his ancestors into the family business.

Zan and her loved each other very much. They had been planning to get married. It had been the happiest time of her life. One cold night, they were walking in their favorite park. A man dressed in a dark suit appeared before them. It was Zan's father. "Why are you planning to get married to her?" his father asked. Zan moving in front of Rose answered, "Because I love her, and she loves me!" His father's face became full of rage. "Love you say. You don't need love. You were promised to the daughter of my friend long before you were born. You would have belonged to the most powerful two families in magic if you would marry her. When I found out that you told her father that you wouldn't marry his daughter, I knew that I had to do something about it."

"You have disgraced all your ancestors. The family always married within their kind. Rose is from a lower class of wizards. She is not from our blood. Her mother is even a Voodoo Priestess. I ask you one more time. Will you forget about marrying Rose and marry who you were promised to?" Zan stood up straighter and looked at his father, Zorn. "I will not. I love my Rose. I renounce the family business. I have other things I want to do!" he shouted back at Zorn. "Then I have nothing for you. I will do what my ancestors before me did to those that didn't honor our family's traditions. I am going

144

to banish you from this world." Before Zan could react, his father said some ancient magic words known only to great wizards. In a puff of smoke, Zan vanished.

She remembered taking out her beads from her pouch and throwing them at Zorn. The exploding beads did not do any damage to him. "You have some powers. I will not kill you. I want to see you suffer the loss of my son as I will. If you ever try to find him, I will kill him and destroy your family," stated Zorn coldly. "Don't worry, someday I will come for you and destroy everything you have. I will find Zan. I will destroy you. You don't know our family's powers. We are a combination of both the wizard world and the voodoo world," she informed him. Zorn laughed at her and vanished before her eyes.

She had looked for Zan for many years. It had been impossible for her to find him. If it hadn't been for Zan's father's return visit to her this spring, she would not have known where Zan was. Zorn had shown her a vision that Zan was alive. In that vision, she noticed a mountain in the vision. It was one she had seen in The Land of the Eagle Feathers. She now knew where Zan was.

What was she to do? She still loved Zan. She loves Nick. If she lost either one of them, it would be too much for her to stand. She remembered the words of a song, *Torn between two lovers*. Her heart was breaking. She knew the only way to find out which one was to find Zan. Did Zan still love her? She knew Nick loved her.

Roses' thoughts turned to other issues. She had other worries. What had happened to the other members of her group? Did they survive the attack by the **Dark Ones**? Is Moses' still in The Land of the Eagle Feathers? Did he survive? What shape is The Land of the Eagle Feathers in? Did it survive the earthquake? What happened to Zan? There were many reasons to be distressed about what had happened. Will they be there when she returns?

Rose took out her crystal ball. As much as she tried, she could not see anything. This dimension was blocking her connection to any other dimension. She had no way of knowing what was happening. Was her whole world in shambles? She worried very much about Nick. How would Nick handle her being gone? She remembered Shanna. Would Nick go back to Shanna, his first love? She knew that she must return for many reasons. Each minute she was here was torture. She had to know what had happened. There was no way to know until she returned. It couldn't come quick enough.

News reached Benita in Houston that her hired killer was dead. She was caught off guard by the news. Her white hair and white skin were striking. Benita didn't like sunlight. She believed it aged people by ruining their skin. In fact, she was somewhat sensitive to the sun. She always wore long dark dresses and hats. Her husband, David, thought the contrast of her white hair and skin to those dark dresses gave her an exotic appearance. She was of medium height and kept herself in great shape by exercise and practicing martial arts. David and she would fight each other until one of them would yield. Their fights were real. They never used protective gear. David liked seeing her bruises against her white skin. She likewise liked to inflict pain on him.

Benita was ambitious. She liked money and especially power. She married David after getting rid of his first wife. David never knew that she was the one responsible for his wife going missing. She took advantage of his pain of losing her. It didn't take long to cast her spell on him. When his wife was declared legally dead, she got him to marry her. He was rich and powerful. She wanted to take credit for her plan to gain control of his empire. She knew his business was dark.

Raven had been the one who approached her about David. Raven, David's Superior or boss, wanted him eliminated. She saw him as a rival. It was Benita's job to get rid of David and take over his business empire.

David's power had grown in the upper levels of **The Omen** which controlled the **Dark Ones**. David wanted to become part of the leadership of **The Omen**. **The Omen** was a group of very powerful mysterious mystics. They controlled many businesses and even countries. **The Omen** used their mystical powers for mostly evil and greed. They wanted to control every aspect of the world's riches.

Benita went to David's office. She had just got back from a fashion show in Paris. The Paris trip had been her cover for the ambush of John's group. David smiled and gave Benita a kiss on her cheek. "Did you have a good trip?" he asked. "Yes, my line of summer and fall fashions were a big hit with the fashion critics. We got many orders. We basically sold out of everything that we can produce," Benita answered with a smile.

David noticed a bruise on Benita's hand. "How did you get this?" he asked. "I took a ride, and the horse threw me. I landed on my arm. I have got other bruises mostly on my back and rear. I would like you to give me a good massage tonight to help with the pain," she said with a wicked smile. Benita knew that would please him. "Why, I would be glad to help my wife in any way I can. Remember that the massage could hurt a little. To take that type of soreness out means I would have to give you a deep massage."

"I cannot wait until tonight. I will have dinner ready for you. When you get home, don't dress for dinner. I will have on my black robe. I will lay out yours. I will see you about 7:30. I will be ready for you," she laughed. David had to say to himself. "It is kind of fun living dangerously. One day, we will part, but not until I get rid of Raven. I need to watch you. Your actions tip me off. When you leave on a business trip, I know

147

you and Raven have something up your sleeve or should I say dress."

Antonio had found the code to which passages in *The Book of Summer* to use to find the clues to where *The Book of Fall* was hidden. He was starting to get excited. *The Book of Fall* would lead to the final book of The Land of the Eagle Feathers which is the powerful *Book of Winter.* It is full of secret and mystical powers. The knowledge that book contains could change the world. It could make him the most powerful man on earth. With a woman like Angela by his side, he would have everything he ever dreamed of and more.

Tomorrow, he had to go to the board meeting at David's Corporate Offices. He would give a short talk about his last trip there. He knew that the Board of Directors members were actually **The Omen**. He would tell them about the rich natural resources. Like David told him, he would throw out a bag of jewels he had collected in the tunnel. There would be one additional item this time. He would show them some nuggets of gold he found. That should be enough to keep their attention.

He was thinking about what to say in the meeting when there was a knock on the door to the office he was using in the museum. He expected to see Rico when he told them to come in. Instead he got a slight surprise as Shanna walked into his office. She was wearing a short summer dress. It showed all her charming features. It definitely was short enough to show off her beautiful long legs.

"What are you doing here?" he asked. "I thought you would like how I am dressed. John wanted me to attend the meeting you have tomorrow as your guest," she answered. "Now, how do I do that? I just can't take you. You must be invited," Antonio stated.

Shanna smiled, "In my hand is an invitation from David. When I told him that Benita tried to kill Lo Ming, he thought you might need a bodyguard. I know that Angela is caught in The Land of the Eagle Feathers. John also sent me to guard you. You may be a good strong boy, but you are no match for Raven and Benita. It takes a woman to outsmart another woman. Besides, I think we would make a cute couple. Don't worry, what I will wear tomorrow will make me look like your assistant. I will wear eyeglasses and a less revealing outfit. I will have my knives on me. Besides, I promised Angela I would take very special care of you. Angela gave me a key to her apartment. She wanted you to have some company if she got detained. See you tonight." Shanna turned and left. Antonio was speechless. He didn't know how to reply to her anyway.

Antonio didn't know what to expect when he arrived back at Angela's apartment that night. Shanna was a beautiful woman. He was tired from all the work he had done on the passages. All he wanted was a good meal and a good night's sleep. He hadn't been sleeping well. He missed Angela. He decided to knock on the apartment's door. He didn't want Shanna to think that he was an intruder. Shanna opened the door. She was wearing one of Angela's loose sweat suits. Apparently, she had just finished working out at the hotel's gym.

"You are a little earlier than I thought. I was about to take a shower after working out. I have our dinner in the oven. It will be done in about 45 minutes. I hope you like chicken with white wine and wild rice. I have roasted some vegetables in garlic and lemon to go with it. There is a pitcher of red sangria I made in the frig. I will join you in a few moments. It won't take me long to take a shower," said Shanna. Antonio decided that he needed to do the same. The guest bedroom had a full bath. He took a quick shower. He looked for something to put on. On the bed was a robe, so he put it on. He was too tired to do anything else. He went out to the kitchen. Shanna had dinner on the table and had poured them some wine. She was wearing one of Angela's lush cotton dark red robes.

They had small talk during the meal. Antonio was impressed with how well the dinner tasted. Shanna had put on some soft music. "You seemed to have gotten along well with Angela," Antonio stated. "Yes, we found we had a lot in common. She is a remarkable woman. She worried about you. I found that refreshing. I thought she was not one for relationships. You are a lucky man to have such a woman interested in you," related Shanna.

"I guess, I am. What about you? I noticed that you have some interest in Nick. I could feel that you two had once had something for each other."

"We did long ago. We met in high school in California our senior year. It didn't last. I went my way, and he went his. It was nice. By the way, I had heard of you before John sent for me. Antonio, you are somewhat of a legend in many circles. I know we have some things in common. You like nice things. You like money. You especially like beautiful women. It takes a lot of money to have a lifestyle like that," stated Shanna.

"I do ok in making money. Sometimes, I have dealt with not the best of characters. I have heard of you, Shanna. My sources say you are a remarkable woman. It is said that you have worked for about anyone that needs your skills. I believe you once worked for the CIA and MI6. How did you get involved with John?" Antonio asked.

"That is a long story. I was in the Middle East doing some business for the firm. I got into a jam. I was to find out some information on some very bad people. They found out. They cornered me in an alley. I thought this was it. I could take on three or four of them, but there were more. John just showed up. He took out four of them with his bowie knife. I don't know how he took out the others. One of them shot me after I took out three in a fight. When I woke up, ten of them were on

150

the ground. He took me to an apartment. He's good at patching people up. I told him. I would repay him. Well, here I am."

"I am tired, Angela, I'm going to sleep in the guest room. Have a good night. I am glad to have met you. You are a good cook. You are beautiful. Angela was right, and you did take good care of me. I will be leaving early in the morning to finish some things. We should leave about 7 tomorrow night for the Board Meeting." Antonio leaned over and gave Shanna a kiss on her cheek and whispered, "Thanks for a lovely evening." He went to bed. It was the first time he had a good night's sleep in several days. Shanna had to say that Antonio could be a gentleman. He must be in love with Angela. One thing was for sure. They were an interesting couple. She wouldn't trust either one of them. That was what she liked about them.

David's secretary buzzed him on the intercom, "You have a visitor. Your daughter is in the office. Should I let her in?" David replied, "Yes, but let her wait until I finish some business."

Mary didn't like waiting. Her patience was running low. She had to have some more information about her past. Finally, David opened the door and let her into his office. She sat down in a big soft black office chair directly in front of his desk. David hadn't expected to see her before the Corporate Meeting that was being held tonight. "What are you doing here?" he asked. "I had to find out some things about my past," she asked. "I told you that I couldn't tell you because of the spell that Benita put on you. You have to find out for yourself," he replied to her. "I have to know more." "Then, I suggest that you have patience and watch Raven and Benita at the meeting tonight. They might say or do something that could jog your memory. I will try to say something to them that might help you. That is all I can do. Remember our plan. We have to

151

make it seem that we know nothing about their attack on your group," said David.

"I know, but I am still troubled by everything. Since my mother is alive, how did you hide that from me all these years?" asked Mary. "I didn't. When she appeared at the meeting, before your group was to leave for finding *The Book of Summer,* I was as shocked as you. I thought she was dead. I always thought that something was not right in her being missing all these years. There was no body ever found. Your stepmother seemed so sure that she was dead. The only thing that was ever found was her car at the town below the Eagle Train Station," answered David.

Mary looked at David. She didn't have to say anything. David knew what she was thinking. "You think that Benita had something to do with her being missing. Don't you?" "Yes, I do. If Raven or Benita stops you from getting the books, they will be able to get you thrown out of being CEO of your Empire. **The Omen** will eliminate you from their organization. Isn't that right, father?" replied Mary. "I will tell you that **The Omen** kills people that do not live up to their standards," David whispered to her.

"I guess. We will have to turn the tables on them," stated Mary. "That means we must get our hands on *The Book of Fall* and follow it to *The Book of Winter.* Our survival depends on it. They will not hesitate to kill both of us including your child," David seriously replied. "What do you want me to do?" asked Mary. "You need to go to the meeting and protect me from them. They might try something. You will have to be careful. Shanna is staying at Angela's apartment. You should go there. It will be safe for you there. You should all come together tonight for your safety," David instructed her.

Mary arrived at Angela's apartment a short time later. She knocked on the door. Shanna asked, "Who is it?" Mary replied, "Mary, David told me to come here and to go to the meeting with you and Antonio for our safety." Shanna let Mary into the apartment. "Well, I guess we will make a nice threesome," Shanna laughed.

Shanna dressed in a black pantsuit with a black jacket. It was low cut, and the pants had a long slit on both legs. Mary had on a dark red empire dress. Antonio decided to wear a black tux with a white shirt and bowtie. They looked fashionable enough for the meeting. Before they left for the meeting, Antonio asked Shanna where her weapons were. Shanna opened her jacket. There were several slits in the underside that had throwing knives in them.

Antonio told her that there might be metal detectors at the entrance to the Corporate Meeting room. "How was she going to get past them?" Antonio asked. "That's easy, I have some Uranium. I put it in the bag you are going to share during your lecture. It will mess up the metal detectors. You will go in first, then Mary and I will follow. Be careful, my sources have detected a large payment for a hit in Houston. I wouldn't be surprised if it was not the meeting tonight," said Shanna.

The corporate limo picked them up at 7 p.m. They arrived at the front of the tall Corporate Building at 7:30 p.m. At the main entrance were two security guards. They had hand held metal detectors. Antonio handed his bag to the first guard. He took his metal detector and placed it on the bag. The metal detector went crazy. The two security guards drew their weapons on them. At that time, they heard a voice say, "Don't worry, they are my guests. I asked them to bring some uranium samples with them. We are thinking of buying a mine. I will take them to the Corporate Meeting." It was David's voice. "Yes, sir," replied the guards.

They took the private executive elevator to the top penthouse floor. David was pleased that his guests looked their part. There were two more guards stationed near the entrance doors to the large meeting rooms. They were both armed. They saluted David and his guests as they opened the doors for them.

The large meeting room had a small stage with a large computer screen behind it. A lecture stand with a microphone was set up on the stage. Three large tables with place mats and table settings were placed in the room. Each table could hold ten guests. Many of the men and women were having drinks or tea and coffee. They were having conversations with each other.

David introduced Shanna to everyone as a new personal assistant and friend of Angela's. Antonio played his part by being his charming self. Mary made it a point to single out Raven and Benita. She talked to them like she missed their company. She made it known to them that she had been studying for a Doctorate in Business Management. When she told Raven and Benita that she planned to take over for David when he retired or died, they both choked on their drinks. Benita gave her a wicked look. Instantly, Mary remembered that look. Her mind remembered a vision of Benita telling her that she was dying. She would never live to have her father's empire. She was going to get it. It was in a jungle that the scene was happening. There were some other scenes as well. She couldn't quite get them in focus.

David had everyone take their seats. He told everyone that Antonio had just returned from The Land of the Eagle Feathers. He was going to give a full report about it before the meal was served.

Shanna looked around the room while Antonio started his lecture. Antonio had the audience spellbound. He not only had one bag of rare jewels and gems, he had three small bags of them. He put one bag of each on a table. He picked one person at each table to open the bag and spill it onto the table. The room lit up with laugher and smiles. Each bag contained priceless jewels and a gray lump of rock. "What is the gray lump of rock?" asked a white-haired man at one of the tables. "I know that you know that there are precious jewels there. The gray rock is something more valuable. It is almost pure uranium. It is more valuable than the other resources in The Land of the Eagle Feathers. I know you will want to know more about it. I suggest that you fund me to go back to The Land of the Eagle Feathers to find out where the large deposits are located."

The Directors all said, "By all means, we think you deserve a bonus for bringing back that information." David got up and said that concludes the presentation. He instructed the caterer to bring in the plates of food and drinks for the banquet.

Shanna immediately knew something was wrong. The food servers were too well built to be normal food servers. It appeared that they had something under their white jackets. They didn't seem to know the best way to serve at each table.

She was about to alert David. Two shots rang out. The two guards outside the meeting room were blasted through the conference doors. A puff of smoke appeared on stage. When the smoke cleared, an older gentleman appeared. By then, several of the food servers had their guns drawn on everyone.

"Let me introduce myself. My name is Kamir. I am from South America. My group wants The Land of the Eagle Feathers. I plan to make sure that your organization does not get this land. To make sure that you don't try to take the land, we are going to take some of you back with us.

Shanna slowly removed two knives from her jacket. She gave them under the table to Antonio. She took out two more. When Kamir's men started to go to pick out who they were going to take, she jumped up and threw both her knives at two different servers. Antonio did the same. All four men fell dead. Two of the gunmen tried to shoot them. Mary stood up with a handgun and shot them down. Two men rushed out of the kitchen door with submachine guns. They took aim at her

155

and Antonio. As one was about to shoot, a rifle shot was heard. He fell down dead. Before Mary or Shanna could throw or fire at the last man, he fired his submachine gun. Shanna instantly jumped on Antonio to protect him. David shot the man with an automatic he had pulled out from under his jacket. Kamir laughed and said, "This means war! We will see who gets the land." In a puff of smoke, he disappeared in front of everyone.

David asked if Antonio was alright. "Yes, I am. Someone needs to help Shanna up. She appears to be wounded." Mary immediately moved over to assist with Shanna. Shanna was bleeding badly from two gunshot wounds. Antonio's tux was covered with her blood. Mary took two cloth napkins and put them on the wounds. She asked someone to call an ambulance. Mary knew that Shanna was hurt so badly that she might not live.

Antonio sat on the floor. He held Shanna in his arms. Shanna looked up at him, "I told Angela I would protect you." Tears were flowing down Mary's face as she tried to stop the bleeding. Shanna passed out.

One of the Directors said he was a doctor. He had a bag with him. "I need to get the bullets out for her to have a chance to live," he said. He opened his bag. He took out two small metal rods. He placed them in the two openings where the bullets went in. He said something in ancient Celtic. It was in Druid language. Antonio knew he must be a Druid priest. The man pulled out the two metal rods from the wounds. Attached to each rod was a bullet. The Druid priest took two red small rocks and placed them over the wounds. He touched them with a small staff that had a large clear crystal on one end. They burst into flames. The flames sealed the wounds shut. "I don't know whether she will make it. This is the best I can do for now. We can't wait for an ambulance. David will need to have a limo take her to a hospital," he said.

Antonio picked up Shanna. He wouldn't let anyone else touch her. With two bodyguards and Mary at his side, he went to the elevator. A black limo was outside waiting for them. They were at the hospital in minutes. Doctors were waiting for them at the hospital. They told them to wait in the emergency room.

David was about to have his men take the bodies away. The bodies burst into flame and turned into dust. The Board of Directors still had their meeting. They told David to stop at nothing until they had control of The Land of the Eagle Feathers. They couldn't let this group led by Kamir get this land. He was powerful. If Kamir got control of The Land of the Eagle Feathers, they would become too powerful for even **The Omen** with their **Dark Ones** to fight.

Raven tried to blame David for the attack. She said that his security was too weak. David looked at Raven, "Someone must have helped them get inside. When I find out who, I will make sure I will deal with them harshly. We must have a traitor in our organization. I will find them." Raven said, "Who shot the man with the submachinegun? It had to be a large caliber to go through the window glass from another building." David answered, "One of my guards stationed outside." Raven knew David was not telling the truth. David knew of only one man that could make that shot. He would never tell Raven it had to be John.

It was a long night for Antonio and Mary at the hospital. After about four hours, one of the doctors came to the waiting room. He told them that Shanna had gone into a coma. They didn't know whether she would live or die. It might be two weeks before she recovers or dies. Antonio and Mary were very upset by the news. They would be needing to leave in one week to get back to The Land of the Eagle Feathers.

After visiting her hospital room, they went back to Angela's apartment. They ordered food and took showers. Antonio's suit was covered with Shanna's blood. Mary had blood on her dress. "Angela's dress is ruined," Mary cried. Antonio knew it wasn't Angela's dress that Mary cried about. "Angela can always get another one. We are lucky to have had Shanna with us. She saved our lives. You never told us that you were packing a gun. You and David saved many lives. The rifle shot saved us all. I wonder who shot that man," Antonio wondered out loud. Mary's mind had visions again. She looked at Antonio. "I once knew of such a man. He was a great marksman. His name was John. I can't seem to visualize his face." Antonio answered back, "I know his face, and you do too."

After getting some sleep, Antonio went back to the museum to complete deciphering the passages. It took a while before he could assign each to a member of the group. Mary returned to the hospital to look after Shanna. She sat by her bedside. David even showed up later. Mary was surprised that David would do such a thing. "The Board of Directors wanted me to notify the hospital that they would cover all the medical expenses for Shanna. They also gave me permission to give Shanna a bonus for saving them," David explained. Mary knew that David could have had his personal assistant do that.

"I cannot prove it. Someone had to have been on the inside to let those men into the building," David told Mary. "I can give you three guesses, and the first two don't count. You know who would gain," Mary angerly said. "Yes, I do," replied David.

Chapter VIII
People got hurt:
Will Shanna survive?

Antonio was satisfied with the work he had done on the passages that he picked for the rest of the members of his group. The passages were getting much more difficult to decipher than the last ones he had done for ***The Book of Spring***. It would have been much easier for everyone if they didn't have to take each book back to the museum in Houston. It would be nice to stay in The Land of the Eagle Feathers. They wouldn't have to worry about those people that wanted to stop them from finding the other books. The Houston museum had some ancient texts that Antonio could consult to assist him in deciphering the books. He had found the passage that gave him clues to which passages to pick for which member of his group to find the hidden clues. Each passage would give clues to where ***The Book of Fall*** was located. This procedure had worked well for them to find ***The Book of Summer***.

The first passage that he deciphered was for Nick. It was called:

For the Love of Your Brother

What would you do
For one other than you
What would you do for another
For the love of your brother

If one piece of bread were left
Would you eat it yourself
If the fight had already begun
Would you leave him and run

If he were drowning in the river
Would you stand there and shiver
If the snake was by his side
Would you run away and hide

If he was attacked by a bear
Would you stand there and stare
If it could cost you your life
Would you be willing to take a knife

No matter who you are
The answers are on the South Star
It tells you what you should do
The rest is up to you.

The next passage surprised Antonio. It was for John. He hadn't expected a passage for him.

Darkness Will Come in the Middle of the Day

Wait to see at the lagoon
Grandfather Sun behind Grandmother Moon
Darkness will come in the middle of the day
Nowhere to run, no words to say

You will not hear a sound
No animals will be around
You must look to yourself
In the end, it's all you have left

You will find yourself alone
Everything you know is suddenly gone
What's left is all in your mind
Everything you know is left behind

You must find a way of survival
You must find a way of renewal
Think before anything you do
My brother, it is up to you

The silence will be all you hear
The loneliness will be all you fear
Nowhere to run, no words to say
Darkness will come in the middle of the day

Antonio was pleased that the next passage was for Moses. He missed that big guy. He couldn't wait to give him this one in person.

The Music of Our Land

If you try to find
Something beyond your mind
You will come to understand
If you listen to the music of the land

Listen to the drops of rain that fall
Listen to the crows that caw
Listen to the song of the wind
Listen to the boughs that bend

Listen to the croak of a frog
Listen to the bark of a dog
Listen to the softness of a horse's sigh
Listen to the pain of a river's cry

Listen to the song of a bird
Listen to all you have heard
Then you will begin to understand
The way to our unknown land

Little brother, only you can hear
You'll know our spirits are near
Little brother, only you can understand
The meaning in the music of our Land

Antonio thought this one was perfect for June. This one he called"

A Tree Without a Leaf

Feel the heat of Grandfather Sun
Remember all that you've done
Watch the light of Grandmother Moon
The Shadow moving of a raccoon

Hear the whisper of the wind
Remember how it's always been
Watch in the middle of a shower
The gentle swaying of a flower

See without opening your eyes
Remember where an eagle flies
Watch in the middle of a storm
The memory of a baby being born

Touch the rock that doesn't feel
Remember all that you thought real
Watch as the eagle flies bye
The rock begins to cry

Look for a tree without a leaf
Remember when you had your belief
It may not all be so
Hey yi, hey yi, hey yi, yo

Antonio knew that this passage was for Lo Ming because it mentioned "a tiger eye."

The Secret to the Way to Our Land

I see said Grandmother Moon
Far beyond the deep lagoon
I hear said Grandfather Sun
Far beyond where the buffalo run

Look up to Father Sky
Watch for the eagle to fly
Look up to Mother Earth
Watch for the signs in the dirt

Look up to the Upper World
Watch for the clouds to swirl
Look down to the Lower World
Watch for the leaves to twirl

Look for the shooting star
It is the center of where you are
Look ahead and look behind
Look inside and outside of your mind

When you find the tiger eye
When the sky begins to cry
You will know and understand
The secret to the way to our land

Mary's passage contains a little bird's nest.

The Little Bird in the Nest

I saw a little bird in the nest
Abandoned by all the rest
He cried out his mama's name
But his mama never came

I said little bird, I'm just like you
I don't know what to do
I'm scared and all alone
Everyone else has already gone

I watched as he chirped to the sky
I knew that he was too scared to fly
It was a long way to the ground
There were no other birds around

I heard his cries for another bird
I knew his cries would not be heard
Just like I cried for you today
There was nothing left to say

I felt the little bird's pain
I knew his cries were all in vain
Left alone by all the rest
I'm like that little bird in a nest

Rose's passage was something of a riddle.

Maybe It's Not What It Seems To Be

Time is a circle spinning around
Down is up, Up is down
Everything you think you see
May not be what it seems to be

West is East, East is West
Maybe it's just a test
Everything you think is near
May not even be here

Earth is water, Water is earth
Birth is death, Death is birth
Everything you think you feel
May not even be real

High is low, Low is high
Maybe you should ask why
Everything you think you know
May not even be so

Birds are us, We are birds
Hear the meaning of our words
Oh, Mother Earth, Father Sky
Hey, yi, Hey, yi, Hey, yi, Hi

Some days later, Antonio would look at the passage that the young Indian woman would give him. It was to tell him how to get back into The Land of the Eagle Feathers.

Which Wolf Will You Feed

In the times of cold and heat
Two wolves inside you will meet
Each one will fight for your soul
Two parts will make a whole

One wolf will only know greed
One wolf will only take what they need
One wolf will only know lust
One wolf will only know trust

You will hear both wolves inside
You will know you can't hide
Each wolf will fight for its place
It's a decision you must face

Nobody else can give you a hand
Nobody else will ever understand
What are you going to do?
When both wolves talk to you

Which wolf will you feed today?
Which wolf will show you the way?
Only you will ever know
Hey, yi, Hey, yi, yo

Each wolf will sing its song
One is right, One is wrong
See with the eye of a sparrow
The answer is in the broken arrow

One night, Antonio took the appropriate passages that he had deciphered to be delivered. He put one in each envelope to be delivered to a specific member of his group. He did not take the passages that belonged to Mary, Rose and Moses. He did what he had done before with the passages from *The Book of Spring*. He went to the old park around the corner from the museum. In the middle of the park was a large Oak tree. He waited there. When the old church clock stuck midnight, he saw her come out of the woods on the other side of the park. A young Indian woman dressed in a short white deerskin dress, riding a painted pony rode up to him.

He gave her several envelopes to deliver. She gave him an old faded brown envelope back. She told him that it was the directions on how to get through the other passage to The Land of the Eagle Feathers. She turned her horse around and galloped to the woods and disappeared.

Nick's grandmother had a frown on her face. Something was wrong. She could sense it. The red sunrise in the east over the mountains confirmed her feelings. She went to Nick's room. Nick asked, "What was the matter?" His grandmother answered, "You need to get your things packed. You need to leave as soon as possible." Nick never questioned his grandmother's feelings. If she said that he needed to leave today, then he needed to leave today. By the look on her face, he knew it had to be bad. He had seen that look before. It usually meant that someone was hurt or dying. "It will take me a few moments to get my things together," he replied in a whisper. Nick was worried.

Nick's grandfather felt me before I arrived. He watched me ride up from the desert floor to the house. "It's been a long time, John. I take this is not a social visit. By the look on your face, it is a bad sign." I nodded my head. "My wife told me you would probably be here today. She could see it in the red sunrise," Nick's grandfather stated. "She always knows when I am coming," I replied. "It's probably because you usually bring bad news," he said to me.

Nick's grandmother came out of the house. "I knew you would be here. What bad news do you have for Nick?" she questioned me. "Nick is needed in Houston. He needs to see an injured friend. He may be the only one that can save her," I told them. "It's Shanna. Isn't it? Nick is getting his stuff together. I have breakfast fixed. You can tell us over breakfast. Then you can leave," she said in an angry tone.

I sat down at the breakfast table. As soon as Nick saw me, he knew that something had happened. "Eat first, then I will tell you. We will have to leave soon after breakfast. A helicopter will be here in an hour to pick you up. David sent it up from Santa Fe. It will take you to the airport. He has a private plane waiting to take you to Houston."

His grandmother and grandfather knew that I was not in the mood for small talk. Nick stuffed his food down. "Now tell me why you are here?" he asked. I looked at Nick. "Before I start, make sure you are calm. You have had a bad time of it. Promise me that you will listen to me. You must keep it together. Shanna needs you to do that," I told him. "Shanna, what happened?" he said with a shocked look on his face. I told them the story about the attempt on Antonio's life. "Shanna was badly wounded. She received two gunshots protecting Antonio. I shot one man, but another got shots off. David killed the man who shot her. She is in the hospital in Houston in the intensive care ward. I won't soften my words. She may not make it. She is in a coma." Nick didn't say a word.

"You are the only one that can save her. This is what you need to do. You must go to the hospital. You need to sit by Shanna's bed. You must tell her the truth about you and her. Talk to her about old times. Tell her stories, she needs to have you bring her back to us. It will take all her strength to come back," I told him.

Nick's grandmother looked at Nick. "I know what you are thinking. How can I bring her back? Only you can say the three magic words to her. If you don't know them, she will die." Nick replied to her, "What words are they?" His grandmother answered, "You will find them, or you are not a grandson of mine."

A horse could be heard outside. A young Indian woman was on a painted pony. She waited for us to come out of the house. She motioned Nick to come to her. She gave him two letters. They were both from Antonio. "Antonio said to read this one before you got to the hospital. The other contains the passage. John, you must take your horse and follow me. We have to talk," she said. I looked at Nick, "You know what you have to do."

As I rode off with the young Indian woman, I saw Nick getting into the helicopter. We rode for about a mile before the trail stopped at a T in the road. "This is where we will part. You will go East. I must go West. I have a message from the other Great Spirits. They are angry at you. They do not approve of the members of your group. They are not pure of heart. They have many flaws in their character. We question their true reasons for obtaining the sacred books. We do not know if we can trust even you. You have much anger inside. You deserve your anger. You have many scars that prove your loyalty. You think that we did not treat you right. That is for us to decide. The Great Spirits have decided that **The Keepers of the Yawi** and you will not get any more help from us. In fact, we will make your next journeys more difficult. You will have to prove your worth."

I chose my reply to her very carefully. "I have given most of my life to The Land of the Eagle Feathers. I have lost many friends protecting it. I do not welcome any help from the Great

Spirits. For many years, I have studied the Mystic Arts and magic. I have the group that will save The Land of the Eagle Feathers. You do not understand mankind. It is our faults that make us. My group have faults. They are human. Each of us have two wolves fighting within us. One is for the good, and one is for the bad. It takes both sometimes to accomplish a quest. We will see which wolf wins. Tell the other Great Spirits that I will use everything in my power to get the books. I have accumulated much knowledge and power over the years. The John that you have known all these years will not be the one that finishes this quest. That is what I have found to be the key. We will only rely on ourselves. Tell them, this will be my last quest for the books. If we fail, it will not matter. I and The Keepers of the Yawi will be dead, and the land will not exist. I will destroy it to keep it from evil."

The young Indian woman replied, "We wish you well. We will be watching you. Your time is running out. Both our times are running out. We are still displeased with some members of your group. The earthquake was our warning. We can only tolerate so much. May the White wolf win over the Black wolf!" I looked at her and saluted her. "I wish you well. We will be needing your services one more time when we get *The Book of Fall.* We will get the books. Nobody will stop us," I told her. "You are so sure with so many against you. There is an Indian saying, "**Your greatness can only be measured by the mightiest of your enemies**." Judging from your enemies, we will find out how great you and The Keepers of the Yawi are." We both turned our horses and rode in opposite directions.

The flight attendant sat down by Nick. She told him that they would be landing in Houston in 30 minutes. There would be a black limo to take him to the hospital. "Shanna is a very brave woman. You need to eat something before we land. I have fixed you lunch. With your help, she will make it. I can feel it.

Remember there are three words that can save her. They must be said by you," she reassured him.

Nick ate his lunch. He opened the letter that Antonio had written to him.

Dear Nick.

I wish I could have written this at a better time. I am not a person that believes in many things. In fact, I am something of a sociopath, they say. I have not cared for many people in my life. For many years, I have lived only for myself. I didn't care who I hurt to get my way. I have learned many things throughout the years in my travels.

I spent a lovely evening with Shanna at Angela's apartment. Shanna is very special. Don't worry, I was a perfect gentleman. I know only one thing. This is very difficult for me to say to you. Shanna loves you very much. She would do anything for you. The reason I can say this is that she made me see that I have the same feelings for Angela. I don't know how this crazy quest is going to turn out. I only know that love like Shanna's only happens once.

Until we meet again,
Antonio

Nick arrived at the hospital about 45 minutes later. He was met by Mary. Mary showed him to Shanna's critical care room. Shanna was still on a respirator. She had tubes everywhere. Nick was not ready for what he saw. Mary told him that it was important for him to talk to her. Shanna needed to hear a familiar voice. It could break her coma. It had been two days since the incident. She was still in critical condition. Mary told him unless she showed improvement soon, they may have to take her off life support. Mary told Nick that she needed to leave. She needed to pick up her passage from Antonio and go to Maine to get some things for the trip back to The Land of the Eagle Feathers. Mary kissed Nick on his cheek and left.

Nick sat down and started talking. He told Shanna that he was not a very good talker or conversationalist. He talked to her about the first time seeing her in history class. He talked in detail about their first date. He surprised himself by remembering all the details including what she wore. It wasn't long before it was getting dark. His voice was getting tired. One of the nurses told Nick to take a break. He didn't want to leave her. The nurse told him they would fix him a place to stay in the room. They asked if she had a favorite song. They laughed when he said, "Born to be Wild." They said they would try to get that song for him to play for her. "It certainly fits her," said the head nurse.

Lo Ming had worked late at her business. Her uncle had left her several ancient mystical magic books to read. It was about 11 p.m. when she left her office to get her car. When she went around to the back of the building, she saw the painted pony. She knew that pony anywhere. The young Indian woman was standing by her car. Lo Ming walked slowly up to the car. "This machine is beautiful. I like the bright red color. By the way, this brown envelope is for you. John wanted me to tell you that Shanna is in critical condition in a hospital in Houston. She was shot protecting Antonio. Nick is there to try to break the coma. There is nothing you can do. Remember to be at the Eagle Train Station in three days. Good Luck, you will need it. Things will get better before they get worse."

The young Indian woman got on her painted pony and galloped around the corner of the building. Lo Ming knew not to follow her. Lo Ming hoped the young woman was right. It was enough to worry about Moses and Rose. Now, she had to worry about Shanna and Nick. Lo Ming would take out her

Tibetan Prayer Wheel and pray for all four of them when she got home.

The sunrise was full of bright colors. June enjoyed watching the bright light make its way across the deep prairie grass. The wind would move the grass in waves like an ocean of green. She was deep in thought when she heard a woman's voice behind her. "Here is your passage from Antonio. I can tell your vision last night told you about what happened to Shanna. When you return to The Land of the Eagle Feathers, you will know that the vision was true. Remember to be at the Eagle Train Station in two days. You need to tell the lesson about the two wolves and the rest of your vision to the others. It is a lesson that they need to learn." Before June could say anything, the young Indian woman turned her painted pony. She rode up and over the high hill behind her.

Antonio went to the hospital to see Shanna and Nick. Shanna was still in a coma. The doctors told them that they needed to take Shanna off the respirator. Nick was beside himself. He had tried everything he could to get Shanna to come out of her coma. He had run out of stories. Antonio told him that they had to leave tonight. David had arranged transportation to the town below the Eagle Train Station. They couldn't be late. They had to leave soon.

Antonio said that he would stay with Nick while they removed Shanna's respirator. He owed that to Shanna and Nick. The doctors removed several of the tubes from Shanna. Finally, they got to the respirator. They told them that if she did not start breathing on her own, she would probably die. Slowly, they took off the respirator. Shanna didn't make any response. She didn't start breathing.

Antonio told him that it was no use. They would have to put it back on her. They had to go. That is when Nick shouted at Antonio, "I can't leave. **I love her.**"

As soon as he spoke those three words, I love her, everything stopped. Nick felt a strange force enter the room. The doctors and nurses were frozen in time. A warm, bright yellow ball of light appeared. It seemed to float in the air. The light settled on Shanna's chest. He could hear voices and then chants from some ancient language. Antonio watched the whole scene before him. The light floated back from Shanna. It moved to the window in the room and disappeared into the night heavens. It became a shooting star. Nick heard his dead mother's voice. "Those words are the most powerful words of all." He could see her face. "This is my gift to you, my son," she said as she faded away. That's when time started again.

Nick and Antonio heard the most beautiful weak voice say behind Nick, "I love you, too." The nurses immediately put an oxygen mask on Shanna. Shanna's eyes had tears in them. They were tears of joy. Nick took her hand in his. "I have always loved you." Shanna moved her mask to the side. She whispered to him, "Go, you must go. I will be here waiting. You have a beautiful mother. We talked." Nick kissed her. The nurses quickly put the mask back on Shanna. Shanna went to sleep. Nick bent over Shanna. He whispered in her ear, holding back his tears, "I don't want to leave you. I will do as you want me to do and leave. I will be back. We will have that special dinner I promised you long ago on the beach. I love you so much."

The doctors told Nick and Antonio that it was a miracle. She shouldn't be alive. However, Shanna was not out of the woods yet. This was a good sign that she could recover. "Don't worry about Shanna. We will take good care of her. You need to go. We always liked her. We will treat her as one of the family," his grandmother said as his grandparents entered the room. "You sure took your time to say the three magic words. Your mother always said they are the three greatest words," his grandmother said with tears flowing down her face. Nick hugged his grandmother. "I saw my mother." "Yes, I know. I did, too," she barely replied.

Antonio took Nick by his arm. "We have to go. You are a lucky man to have such a family. I agree with Shanna. Your mother is beautiful." Nick wiped the tears from his eyes. He reluctantly followed Antonio to the waiting limo.

During the limo ride, Nick was quiet. That was fine with Antonio. Antonio had his own thoughts. What he had just seen reminded him of his own feelings about Angela. He knew that he loved her. He prided himself as one that would always be in control. This was new to him. He had no control over his feelings for Angela.

Did she feel the same way about him? He didn't know the total answer to that question. What he did know was that she must because Shanna would never have promised her to protect him. There was something he remembered in the way Shanna said to him, "I promised Angela I would protect you." Shanna was almost happy that she did, even though she was dying. He would never forget those words. He smiled. He had his answer.

Antonio could sense that Angela was in some kind of trouble. He just felt it. He had to get back to her. He took out his wallet. He opened it and held in his fingers a lock of Angela's hair. Yes, he could feel she was in trouble. He whispered to himself. "I am coming, Angela. I am coming." Nothing was going to stop him from getting to her.

It was a rainy day in Houston. David was alone in his office. He had received from the hospital the news that Shanna might survive. She had saved him twice. It wasn't that that bothered him. He had seen how Shanna looked at Nick. Someone once looked at him the same way. His thoughts were on the group especially Mary. Was he really a grandfather? After locking his office door, he put on an old record and looked out at the rain. He poured himself a stiff drink of fine Kentucky bourbon and stared out the window. The raindrops on his office window reminded him of tears. "I remember that when it rained, you would always say even the sky was crying. I thought you were dead. I'm playing our favorite song. It was the only time in my life that I was happy." He unlocked a hidden safe in the wall and took out a picture. It was a picture of the Red Woman.

Chapter IX
The Journey Back:
Which way to go in?

I rode up to the Eagle Train Station on my white horse. Sitting in a rocking chair was the old man with his old hound dog. "Get off that horse and come down and sit awhile, John," said the old man. I dismounted my horse and hitched it to the rail. I sat down in a chair next to him. "What's on your mind, old man?" I asked. The old man took a bite of some chewing tobacco. "Are you not a little early for Fall to be going up the mountain?" he pointed out. "I guess you are missing some of your crew. At least two by my count, the big fella and the one that looks like a gypsy. You think you can find them?"

I looked at the old man, "That's why I'm here. The others are coming pretty soon. They should be on the train late tonight. Could you fix them some food and coffee or tea?" The old man replied, "Do I look like a caterer? I guess so. I get a kick out of listening to them talk. That Antonio is a talker. He likes beautiful women. That one girl of his, Angela, is a looker. She went up the mountain about three weeks ago and hasn't come back. I bet you are looking to find her too. You seem to lose a lot of people lately."

The old man spit some tobacco juice into an old coffee can. "I know you will be trying that old way of getting into those mountains. I advise against it. It is too dangerous. I would try the tunnel way first, but that is not up to me." I wondered how he knew so much about my business. "I will do as the spirits say to do. We will soon find out which way to go," I replied to him. "My advice to you, John, is to do what you think is best. Remember you are fighting humans. They are hard creatures to figure. Sometimes those Great Spirits tend to forget that. That group of yours is the best thing I ever saw. They know how to fight humans or creatures because they can think like them. It sometimes takes one to beat one. You must think like a black wolf to catch a black wolf. You listen to that Antonio feller. If I had to catch a black wolf, I'd take him any day. Him and Angela are the same like two peas in a pod. You had better watch them."

"You are right, old man. Do you have the food I asked for? I will be back in the morning. I got something to do tonight." I said back to him. The old man picked up the cloth sack next to him. He handed it to me. "That should be enough for tonight. There are some oats for your white horse in there as well. One other thing is about that white woman, Mary. You and she would make a fine couple. It will take you awhile to get her on your side, if she doesn't kill you first. Have a good day, John," the old man spit another round of juice into the can.

Nick felt the crystal on his necklace start to feel warm. He unbuttoned a couple of his buttons on top of the shirt. He watched as the crystal turned purple. He was relieved Rose was alright. She would be back for the journey for *The Book of Fall.* He wondered how he was going to handle his situation now that he knew he loved Shanna. The more he thought about Rose, the more he knew that she had been good for him. The last time he was with Rose, he could sense something was different about her. He decided that he would have to handle this carefully. He would first ask her about why she seemed distant to him. Rose wasn't telling him something. He would play this one by ear.

It was about midnight when they all boarded the old red passenger car. Mary, Lo Ming, Antonio and Nick took their seats. The old train engine puffed its way up the old tracks towards the Eagle Train Station. They had put their gear in the boxcar behind them. The old conductor took their tickets that John had left them. He said, "I see that you are still alive. You have made it farther than any other group that John took to the mountains. There was another group that did well, but they had to quit because some of them got hurt or died. Several of you look like some of them."

The old man and his hound dog had got the food ready for their late-night guests. The train arrived about 3 o'clock in the morning. The old conductor told them to go and get something to eat. He would leave their belongings in the old train station. "Good luck, you will need all you can get. Hope to see all of you on my return trip," as he bid them fair well.

They went to the old hotel. Inside they found a good meal already set for them. There were hot biscuits, gravy, eggs, fruit and sweet breads with coffee and tea. When they finished their breakfast, they went to the train station to change their clothes and meet John. At the train station, the old man was guarding their belongings with his old hound dog. "You came back a little early," he said. "John will be back a little later in the morning. He said he had something he had to do. I put some extra rocking chairs on the porch for you to wait. I know that you want to hit the trail as soon as possible. Until daylight, you can't do anything anyway."

The old man noticed that the group was not very cheerful. He understood why. They seemed to be uneasy. They had their weapons already out as if they were expecting trouble. The group watched the sunrise. The mountain mist was turning different colors. In the distance, a small thunderhead was flashing lightning. This created a cool breeze. It was a pleasant morning.

The old man asked, "Would anyone want to help me pack the mules and saddle the horses?" June answered, "I got to have something to do. This waiting around is killing me. I want to find out about my friends." Everyone commented that they felt the same. June, Mary and Antonio volunteered to assist him.

Lo Ming had decided to talk to Nick. She asked Nick to stay with her. "I understand Shanna may recover. That is good news," said Lo Ming. "I know now why it was best for Moses not to come back with us. I found out that a hired killer was out to get him. His name was Mr. Omega," said Lo Ming. Nick noticed that Lo Ming used the word "was." "I take it that you made sure that Moses wouldn't have to worry about him. He is a very deadly man. I had a run in with him once. We both got cut up. Moses is a very good warrior, but he is a warrior. Mr. Omega is not a warrior. He is an assassin. I take it you killed him." No, I didn't. His mother, Li Ching, did," added Lo Ming. Nick whistled, "Now that's a great martial artist. I have heard she only had one person that she never beat. I have a feeling that person was you. Moses is lucky to have two great martial artists by his side. I hope Rose and Moses are alright. I got a sign about Rose." Nick showed her. "Moses will be alright. I won't have it any other way," said Lo Ming.

John arrived at the old corral about 10 a.m. His white horse looked like he had ridden it pretty hard. It was sweating. "I will need to give my horse a little breather." He took one look at the group in front of him. "My horse will recover fast. Judging by the looks of you, we need to hit the trail. Give him 20 minutes. The old man will give you some snacks to eat. I don't think you can wait much longer."

It was about 10:30 a.m. when the group left the Eagle Train Station. They were making good time. Up ahead, they heard a voice coming from around a bend in the trail. "It's about time you all showed up. I was getting mighty lonely out here," yelled Rose. When they came around the bend in the trail, there

179

sat Rose on her red stallion. She had on a long red dress that covered her saddle. Nick went straight up to her. "We were worried sick about you. How did you get away from the **Dark Ones**?" he asked. "Well, that's a long story. I took them to another dimension, and my friends and I took care of them. They won't be back," she stated in a frank manner.

I tossed Rose some health bars and told her to fall in line. We stopped at the hot springs several hours later to camp. Nick and Rose cooked the evening meal. They were talking to each other like two old friends that hadn't seen each other for years. I told everyone that we would get a very early start tomorrow. We would have to decide which way to go. There is a fork in the trail that leads two ways. One way is the way we have been going, and the other is the hidden way. We will have to decide when we get there. I noticed that Rose and Nick had pitched their tents together.

I asked June to have her black wolf, Midnight, stand watch. She thought that was a great idea. June and her wolf played together for a short time before we went to our tents. I saw Antonio looking at one of the passages he had deciphered. "What's wrong, Antonio?" I asked him. "The passage I got from the young Indian woman seems to have a hidden message in it. It's like a riddle. I will have to study it some more tonight," he replied.

Nobody said anything, I could tell that they were sensing something was out of place. June said something about the evening being too quiet. "I don't hear any birds or animals," she pointed out. "Yes, I have noticed that. We should be safe tonight. Keep your weapons close to you anyhow. Remember no modern weapons work here except Black powder ones," I reminded everyone. I put my white stallion in front and June's wolf behind the camp. They would give us warning if anyone or thing was near.

It was about midnight when I heard Midnight growl and my white horse making noise. I grabbed my Hawken rifle and rolled out of my tent. A white flash went from one side of the clearing to the other. We heard several men shout that they were hit. Another flash of lightning went over us to our front. Again, we could hear a number of men shouting. Finally, a flare was shot straight up above us. It lit up the clearing and woods. Antonio had his wand and shot a stream of light at two of the men coming toward us. Nick put his hands together and formed a ball of fire and threw it at several men gathered at the other side of us. Several loud explosions rocked the clearing. One going off after another moving in a circle around us.

Another flare was shot up. The men could be seen running away from us. Rose threw a few of her exploding beads to hasten them on. She laughed. Mary asked, "What was so funny?" Rose smiled with her bright teeth showing, "John set us up. He knew someone was going to come at us tonight. He set some small charges in the woods with tripwires. They didn't hurt anyone. They were to scare them off. I had seen him riding hard down the trail earlier today."

Lo Ming asked, "Who was the one that warned us?" The answer to that came with a howl of an old hound dog. "Well, I guess that was me," said the old man with his dog. I saw some men in the woods last night. I followed you, knowing that they would take the first chance they could get to ambush you. I was right. Now get a good night's sleep. I'm going home. By the way they were running, they won't be back anytime soon. I did enjoy myself. There's one thing I want you to know, I don't know who attacked you. They are new to these parts. Be careful," he said as he spit his chew of tobacco on a nearby rock. He turned and walked into the night. Everyone just stared after him and thought, "Who is he?"

Nick wasn't too happy with me for not telling anyone about my trick. All he said with a smile, "With friends like you, John, who needs enemies?" Rose and he went back to their tent. I told the others to get some sleep. We would leave in about four hours. I checked the horses. They had settled down.

Nick and Rose had been talking. She could sense that something was different about Nick. Nick seemed at peace with himself. Nick also could sense that Rose had been holding something back from him. "Rose, did you ever have someone that was close to you, and you lost them?" he asked her. Rose replied that she had lost someone very dear to her. "Did you ever find out about what happened to them?" he asked again. "Yes, in a way, I did," she answered. "Did you ever wish that they would come back to you?" he asked again. "More than you would ever know," she whispered back. "I know how you feel, Rose." Nick replied. Before Nick could say anything more, Rose said, "It's Shanna. Isn't it?" Nick answered, "Yes."

Rose was not surprised. She knew when she could see Nick in her crystal ball that Nick was not going to be the one for her. Nobody could ever see their true love through a crystal ball because it would mean that you were using magic for their own gain.

"You and I have a special bond. I have not been totally truthful to you. I have a first love like you. His name is Zan. He was taken from me long ago. I have just found out he is alive. His father placed him somewhere in The Land of the Eagle Feathers to hide him from me. I don't know where. His father is a very powerful Wizard. I will need help to find him and bring him back," she stated with tears in her eyes. "That was why you were so distant on the last trip back to land," said Nick.

"I saw you talking to Antonio earlier. He told you about Shanna. I knew that you knew. I had to tell you the truth. I owe so much to you, Rose. You helped me through some rough times. You know that I will do anything to help you. I will help you find Zan, and we will deal with his father." Rose hugged Nick and said, "Now I know why John sent me your dog tags. I was to help you. We were to help each other. You were a great comfort for me." Rose reached into a bag by her sleeping bag. She pulled out two dog tags that were in bad shape and handed them to Nick. "I believe these are yours."

I got the group up before dawn. We had a quick meal of oatmeal. We were on the trail before light. There was no sign of whoever tried to attack us last night. I took them another way up the mountain to save time. It was very difficult for the horses. We had to be very careful. It would save us a day's walk. Morning Star met us in a small meadow about 3 in the afternoon. We gave her our horses and left on foot for the rest of the way. We ate some health bars for a snack. Everyone had only one thing on their mind. We must get into The Land of the Eagle Feathers. We must find Moses, Angela and One Feather.

It was starting to get dark when we got to the T in the trail. One way went to the tunnel, and the other way went to the hidden way to get into The Land of the Eagle Feathers. I looked at Antonio. "Well, unless someone says different. We will go the other way instead of the tunnel to get into the land," I stated to everyone. Antonio put up his hand, "I am not so sure that is the way to go. I have the passage that would help us go the new way, but something seems wrong with it. It is like it's trying to tell me something about which way to go." "What do you mean Antonio?" Mary asked.

"There is something in the last stanza that makes me believe that we need to think about it," answered Antonio. "What did that stanza say?" asked June. Antonio repeated it for her.

Each wolf will sing its song
One is right, One is wrong
See with the eye of a sparrow
The answer is in the broken arrow

June made the call of a sparrow. She whistled. Soon, a small sparrow appeared. It flew and landed on the boulder near the middle of the T in the trail. June looked at the boulder. It had a broken arrow carved into the stone of the boulder. June shook her head. She stated, "Usually, a broken arrow is bad luck. I wouldn't go toward where the arrow pointed." Antonio thought for a moment before he looked at everyone and stated, "No, that is what the passage is telling me. The sparrow looked in the direction of the broken arrow's point. **See with the eye of the sparrow, the answer is in the broken arrow** means to go in the direction of the broken arrow. That is the opposite of what most people would do. We need to go to the tunnel. If we go in the other direction, we will not get through to the land."

I looked at Antonio, "If Antonio feels strongly about that way, then we should go that way. The old man said something about going that way two nights ago. I told him he was wrong. I guess he knew better than me. We will do as Antonio says." As if to emphasize that Antonio was right, a black dog appeared on the trail to the hidden passage. He was barking and growling. Rose said, "Where I come from, a black dog in your path means to go the other way or something bad will happen." It didn't take any more convincing for everyone to head for the tunnel.

Antonio took the lead toward the tunnel. We looked for signs of anyone using the trail. There were no signs. It took us three hours to get to the tunnel's opening. Antonio looked at the ancient words on the stone beside the tunnel. They change every time the tunnel closes. Antonio said the meanings to the words, "We come to help The Land of the Eagle Feathers. Let us go to save this sacred land from those who will destroy it." The boulders that sealed up the tunnel to The Land of the Eagle Feathers moved. We ran through the opening before it sealed itself back.

We lit our torches and started to move down the tunnel. I knew that everyone was thinking about how were we going to move all the rocks that blocked the other end of the tunnel? We soon got our answer. When we arrived at the blocked passageway out of the tunnel, there was a short stick with a note on it. Mary took the note and read it to us, **"I knew you would need some help. I have put enough charges of dynamite around the rocks to move them out of your way. Light the fuses and run back to the bend in the passageway until it explodes. Then you will find you way out. Good Luck!"** Mary said that there was not any signature on the note. I took the note from her. On the bottom of the note was a brown smudge of tobacco. Lo Ming saw it too. "The old man must have done this. See the tobacco smudge. That's his way of signing it."

There was nothing else we could do but light the fuses. We ran back to the bend in the tunnel and waited. The whole mountain shook when the blast sounded from the dynamite. Dust was everywhere. We made our way back to the area that was blocked. The tunnel was open. You could see daylight on the other side.

June stood between us and the opening. **"Before we go out of the tunnel to The Land of the Eagle Feathers, I must give you a message from the great spirits. I was given a vision that said that we have two wolves inside of us. One wolf is good; one wolf is bad. The Great Spirits feel that most of us are fighting and feeding the wrong wolf. They blocked the tunnel and caused the earthquake. It was to warn us that we must feed the good wolf. There is another thing about my vision. The Great Spirits said that they are punishing the land. They feel that we are not respecting the ancient ways. They made the earthquake much bigger. They said they would try to protect our friends. They didn't say they would."**

Antonio, Lo Ming, Mary, Nick, Rose and June couldn't wait any longer. They had waited three weeks already. They ran for the opening in the tunnel. They fell to the ground just short of

185

the opening. They were in great pain. There was a great sense of despair in their voices. It was as if everything they feared had come crashing down at once. I ran to see what they saw. I could see tears running down their faces. I looked at the scene before us. I could hear it in their crying voices. It was like someone had torn their hearts out. They kept saying, "No! No! What are we going to do now?" After looking at the scene before us, I could only whisper, "I don't know. I have never seen anything like this. How could have they survived?"

Everyone was soon silent. June's black wolf appeared by her side. Her wolf said it all with one mournful howl for her mate. That mournful howl seemed to echo a million times throughout The Land of the Eagle Feathers. As the last echo faded, the silence became deafening.

About the Authors:

Joe G. Morin was born and raised on a small rural farm. He currently lives in East Tennessee where he taught Adult Education for several years. His ancestors came from Tennessee, Kentucky, and Virginia. His current publications on Amazon.com are *Why Men Have Problems with Women and An Angel in the Kitchen.* He loves to tell stories. He is from a family of story tellers. He would listen to his Grandfather tell his stories about being a rural school teacher and farmer for hours. You may contact him at joegmorin@gmail.com

Jo Ann Bullard was born in East Tennessee. Having been a professional entertainer, she traveled all over the world. There is no place like East Tennessee. She lives and writes in the foothills of the Smoky Mountains. Her ancestors were Cherokee, Blackfoot and Scotch-Irish. Her current publications on Amazon.com are *The Problems with Men, and An Angel in the Kitchen.* She has written several articles for professional publications. She is currently working on a volume of song lyrics. You may visit her at ja2bullard@gmail.com

This Book is second part of series about The Land of the Eagle Feathers.

The following is the order of the series called: The Land of the Eagle Feathers.

The Land of the Eagle Feathers: The Book of Spring

The Land of the Eagle Feathers: The Book of Summer

The Land of the Eagle Feathers: The Book of Fall

The Land of the Eagle Feathers: The Book of Winter

The Book of Winter is the final ending of the series.

For those that would like the series with the adult scenes taken out. These are the same books except start with: The Quest of the Land of Eagle Feathers.

The Quest of the Land of the Eagle Feathers: The Book of Spring